KT-168-095

HUNTING GAME

Also by Helene Tursten

Detective Inspector Huss
Night Rounds
The Torso
The Glass Devil
The Golden Calf
The Fire Dance
The Beige Man
The Treacherous Net
Who Watcheth
Protected by the Shadows

An Elderly Lady Is Up to No Good: Stories

HUNTING GAME

HELENE TURSTEN

Translated from the Swedish by Paul Norlen

First English translation published in 2019 by
Soho Press
853 Broadway
New York, NY 10003

Library of Congress Cataloging-in-Publication Data
Tursten, Helene, author.
Norlen, Paul R., translator.

Hunting game / Helene Tursten ;
translated from the Swedish by Paul Norlen.
Other titles: Jaktmark. English

I. Title

PT9876.3.U55 K3513 2018.839.73'8—dc23.2018016750

ISBN 978-1-61695-650-9
eISBN 978-1-61695-651-6

Printed in the United States of America

10 9 8 7 6 5 4 3 2 1

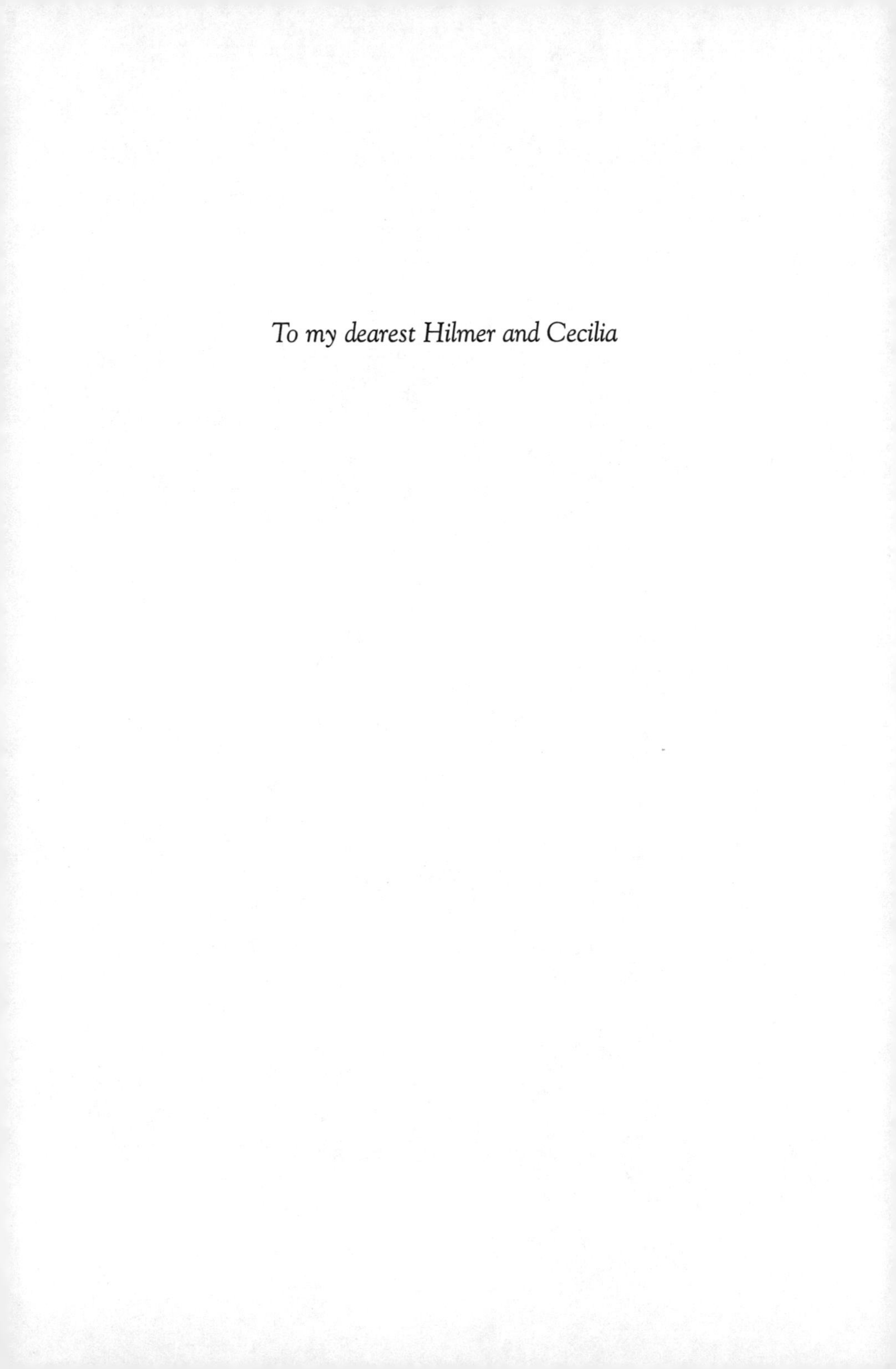

To my dearest Hilmer and Cecilia

After nine rock-hard rounds, the sweat was dripping from both combatants and their movements were noticeably slower. The boxer in the red-and-white top tried a few attacks against the opponent's stomach but couldn't make a solid hit. The boxer in blue and yellow immediately rallied and answered with a quick series of short jabs against the red-and-white's leather helmet to the heated shouts of the spectators. A few of the hits landed solidly, and one made the opponent stagger. The match was even and the outcome uncertain.

When the gong sounded the referee blew the whistle, and the fighters went to their respective corners of the ring. They spit out mouth protectors, and the trainers gave them dry towels to wipe themselves with. Both drank some water but poured most of it over their faces to revive themselves.

The boxers were called up and stood on either side of the referee. He took their hands and held them along his sides until the three judges reported their scores. When he raised the victor's arm toward the ceiling, an ear-splitting cheer broke out.

"Embla Nyström is the new Nordic light-welterweight

champion!" a voice announced, barely audible over the audience's ovations.

All the new gold medalist heard as she raised her arms toward the ceiling was the acclaim of the crowd. In the rush of victory, she felt neither fatigue nor pain. Smiling happily, she stood in the middle of the ring and let the cheers wash over her.

After a glance at her face, the trainer started carefully guiding Embla in the direction of the locker room. She was bleeding above one eye and had to wipe blood away several times with the towel. It didn't bother her in the least; she was radiantly happy.

THE SECRETARY SLIPPED quietly through the doorway with a small tray in her hands and set it down discreetly on the antique mahogany desk. Beside it she placed the day's mail in a neat pile before slipping out again. Anders von Beehn nodded curtly in thanks and continued his phone call.

For a long time he listened to the voice from the other side of the Atlantic. Finally he stretched in his chair and said, "Yes, I'm looking forward to seeing you in New York, too. Bye."

When he hung up his smile faded. Doing business with Americans was quite different than it was with Europeans. Yankees may sound easygoing, but he knew not to let himself relax. After many years at the top of the Swedish business world he was no fledgling and felt rather certain that he would succeed in pulling off the deal. In just a few more months, Scandinvest would be at the top of the list of Sweden's most successful family-owned companies.

A few days off during moose-hunting season felt well deserved; he had been working hard on this cooperation agreement. The low-key trip to the hunting cabin was just what he needed to wind down and get a fresh burst of energy before the final negotiations.

He always opened his personal mail after morning coffee, and a small padded envelope caught his attention. He picked it up and assessed its weight in his hand. He squeezed it carefully. Hard and lumpy. *How strange*.

He set it down gently on the desk and pressed the intercom. "Was the padded envelope X-rayed?" he asked.

"Yes. It's a key chain."

Anders von Beehn slit open the envelope and peeked inside. He reached in and fished out a key ring with no keys. He recognized the BMW logo inside the plastic ring at once.

He sat there a long time, looking at the key ring. What was the meaning? Advertising? A joke? He had a hard time seeing what was funny. Over the years he'd had several BMWs. And a lot of other makes, too, for that matter. Right now the family owned four cars, one of which was actually a new BMW, which his wife, Linda, drove.

When he turned the envelope upside down and shook it, a slip of paper came floating out and settled on the shiny desktop. He read it several times without understanding a thing.

I remember. M.

M? He noted that the text on both the note and the envelope was printed, not handwritten.

Who was M? Suddenly he felt the coffee churning in his stomach. M. That wasn't possible, was it? Was someone trying to mess with him? Trying to scare him? Who knew about M? Jan-Eric, naturally. But he would never do anything like this. He had never even wanted to talk about it. No, not Jan-Eric. Who? Ola. But Ola was dead.

THE AUTOMATIC GATES slowly closed behind the heavy motorcycle. The driver braked with the engine on idle. He unlocked the mailbox on the inside of the wall and emptied it. He stuffed the letters inside his motorcycle jacket before he stepped on the gas and continued down the lane with its newly planted trees.

Whistling, he unlocked the door that led into the house from the garage. Purposefully he guided his steps toward the kitchen. Or rather the refrigerator. Sitting with a couple of beers in the warm Jacuzzi was part of his usual evening routine. If he had the energy he would also swim a few laps in the big pool. Nowadays his body got stiff after a longer motorcycle ride. *You're starting to feel that you'll be turning fifty in a few months*, he thought, grimacing at his reflection in the glass door to the patio. Money can take care of many things, but the passage of time can't be stopped. He carefully drew his hand across his thinning hair.

No, he wasn't going to get gloomy now. It was Friday evening, tomorrow he would pack for the moose hunt and later in the afternoon drive to Dalsland. He was truly looking forward to Saturday's traditional hunting dinner.

He tossed the mail on one of the gleaming stone

counters. He opened the brushed-steel refrigerator, took out a can of Czech beer, and opened it. As always just hearing the fizzing sound filled him with pleasure.

He opened the patio door wide and went out onto the large deck. With a deep breath he drew the fresh autumn air into his lungs. When he went in to get another beer his eyes fell on the letters. Might as well open them before he got into the Jacuzzi along with a few more beers.

From the magnetic holder over the stove he took down a sharp Japanese steel knife and quickly slit open all the envelopes. One of them gave him pause. It was a small, square, padded envelope. His name was printed on a label: *Jan-Eric Cahneborg*. He turned the envelope over, but there was no return address.

Puzzled, he pulled out a thin, black piece of fabric that was inside. It took a few seconds before he realized what it was. A bandanna? He peeked into the envelope to see if it contained anything else. At the bottom he glimpsed a small slip of paper. With some difficulty he managed to coax it out. The text was printed out from a computer.

I remember. M.

Jan-Eric Cahneborg gasped. His facial color changed to a sickly grayish white, and he had to support himself against the granite counter.

Sunset turned the white facade of Dalsnäs Manor a shade of pink. A clear, sunny autumn day was coming to an end. Anders von Beehn looked at the weather forecast for the next three days. Temperatures below freezing were predicted at night, with some chance of sun during the days but no warmth, three degrees above freezing max. Cold, but promising. It was important that the hunt be successful, especially since Volker Heinz was coming. Heinz was the owner of DEIGI, one of Germany's largest investment companies and Scandinvest's most important European partner. Besides that, he was a key player in the negotiations with the US because he had been landing deals with the Americans for a long time. Von Beehn had also invited Scandinvest's lead attorney, Lennart Folkesson. He was a smart strategist and together they could probably handle the good Heinz.

Within half an hour three new luxury cars were gleaming on the well-raked gravel roundabout in front of the manor. A short distance away was a Hummer H3 Alpha. The big car was von Beehn's pride. He had imported it directly from the US. The Hummer was extended, classified as a limousine, and could take eight passengers with no problem. The back seats could be laid flat when you needed extra room for your baggage. As he liked to say, the engine drank gas as if someone had fired a hail of large-bore buckshot into the fuel tank, but the heavy car could go anywhere and was built like a small tank, which was a prerequisite for navigating the roads up to their destination: the Hunting Castle, as they had taken to calling it. The Hummer was used only for transport during the hunt; otherwise it was parked in the garage at Dalsnäs. Now his new Jaguar XJR was parked there instead. It would have been nice to have it out on the yard, too, simply to show off its beauty, but it would have been a bit cramped.

Last of all Greger Liljon skidded in front of the steps with his new Maserati. The young man, who was recently appointed as CEO of one of Scandinvest's smallest companies, was hanging on a slender thread. Greger was surely aware of his standing, but von Beehn intended to speak with him about it after the hunt. The most recent quarterly reports had been catastrophic. Actually it was Greger who was the catastrophe. *Incompetent*, von Beehn thought, but he did not let his face betray his thoughts. With a warm hug, he welcomed his nephew.

The host escorted his guests through the hall and up the broad stairs to the upper floor, where the doors to the terrace were open. They stepped out to admire the view of the lake. The last rays of the sun glistened on the slightly rippled surface. Here and there a bright red maple blazed among the deciduous trees ringing the lake.

As beautiful as an ad, von Beehn thought contentedly. Smiling, he handed a glass of champagne to each of the guests. Once everyone was holding a glass he said in impeccable English, "Dear friends, welcome to Dalsnäs. Cheers to a good moose hunt!"

He raised the champagne flute and the sun's last streak of light reflected in the cut crystal. The others followed his example, nodded to each other, and toasted.

When everyone had taken a sip von Beehn cleared his throat.

"Last year the three musketeers were on the scene. We've stayed together for more than forty years, Jan-Eric, Ola, and me. This year Ola is no longer with us." He turned to Volker. "To fill you in, he died in a car accident as he was driving home to Oslo after last year's moose hunt here at Dalsnäs. Our friend leaves behind a big hole that is impossible to fill. I want to make a toast to the memory of our friend and comrade Ola Forsnaess. To the memory of Ola!"

Everyone raised their glasses again, this time with serious expressions. They sipped the champagne, and the conversation was subdued for a few minutes. Volker Heinz was the only one of the men on the terrace who had never met Ola Forsnaess. Obviously he, too, was moved by the emotional speech, but after a while he started talking with the others about things more near at hand, like the impending hunt. His enthusiasm and hopes were contagious, and an expectant mood spread on the terrace. When the last drop of champagne was swallowed and the sun had long since disappeared behind the hills, they went in and sat down to dinner.

AFTER DINNER THE gentlemen moved to the library. The fire had started to die down but Anders fed it some sturdy logs, and soon a blaze was roaring in the open fireplace. The flickering light from the flames made the gold foil on the leather spines shine behind the glass doors of the bookshelves. Sated and content, they sat comfortably submerged in the English Chesterfield furniture. The whiskey they drank had been aged for eighteen years. Excellent, they were all in agreement about that, especially Jan-Eric Cahneborg, who enthusiastically requested refills several times.

When Anders went out into the kitchen to get another bottle, Jan-Eric followed him on unsteady legs.

"Anders . . . listen . . . we need to . . . talk." He spit out the words as he stumbled.

"Not now, Janne."

"It's im . . . important!"

The desperation in Jan-Eric's voice was clear. He swayed as he stood in the middle of the kitchen.

"A bandanna . . . a fucking ban . . . danna . . . who sent . . . who would send . . . such a thing?" he said, hiccoughing.

Anders almost sobered up when he heard what his friend was saying. "Did you get something in the mail?" He started to feel the burning pain in his stomach again. He recalled the key ring with the BMW logo and the little slip of paper that had floated out of the padded envelope.

"Of course you . . . understand. An envelope . . ."

With the new bottle in one hand Anders went up to his friend and took firm hold of his upper arm with his free hand and guided him toward the library. "We'll talk about this later," he hissed in his friend's ear.

THE GRAVEL SPRAYED around the tires of the Volvo 245 as Embla did a donut on the farmyard before coming to a stop, as she always did when she pulled into Nisse's place. It was her way of signaling she had arrived. The move always made her uncle chuckle with delight, saying, "Here comes hot-rod girl" as she barged into his otherwise peaceful existence. The first time he had said that, Embla had been fifteen and had "borrowed" her brother's moped and driven all the way from Gothenburg. En route she had spent the night with a cousin and his family outside Vänersborg. She never would have made it otherwise. The soreness in her rear padding had persisted for several days. When she was going home again, her uncle had lowered the back seat in his Volvo 245, loaded the moped into the cargo space, and driven her home to Gothenburg.

Three years later he had given Embla that car when she got her driver's license.

She'd had the car for ten years, and at this point it had almost three hundred thousand kilometers on it. Even though the car was starting to show a few signs of old age, Embla loved it. The most serious complaints were that the speedometer was unreliable and the fuel gauge didn't work. After running out of gas a few times in the middle of nowhere, she always had a full can of gas with her when she drove long distances.

As Embla got out of the car she heard Seppo's loud barking coming from the back of the house. Because he didn't come rushing around the corner she figured the Swedish elkhound must be in the dog run.

The front door opened wide and Nisse came out on the steps with a broad smile and outstretched arms.

"Hey there, hot-rod girl!"

He gave her a bear hug. She drilled her nose into his blue checked flannel shirt and took in the scent of barn and sweat. The smell of Nisse, her beloved uncle who was made of the same robust stuff as her mother, Sonja, and herself. Like his sister, he'd had a red, curly mop of hair in his youth. Nowadays only Embla and the youngest of her three brothers retained the family's striking hair color. Sonja's and Nisse's hair had turned gray, and as far as her uncle was concerned, there was almost nothing left on the top of his head. It hardly bothered him because he kept it cut short with his electric razor. It suited him and gave him a tough look.

"And the Veteran keeps on chugging," he said, giving the car a tender pat on the hood.

"You bet. Runs like a clock!"

That wasn't quite true but Embla knew that was what her uncle wanted to hear. The Volvo was the apple of his eye. He was also the one who had christened the car. At first she thought it sounded silly, but now she referred to it as the Veteran, too.

"Settle in while I take a shower and tidy up. As usual we're going to see Karin and Björn," he said.

Karin was the only one of her cousins who was still living in the village. She is Nisse and Sonja's older sister's daughter. Her aunt and uncle had lived in Uddevalla for almost twenty years now. There they had worked in their one son's retail nursery, but now they were both retired. They felt at home on the coast and intended to stay there.

Even though Karin was five years older than Embla, the two cousins had spent quite a bit of time together on summer vacations. Karin also had older brothers—though only two—so over the years, they each became the sister the other had always wished for.

Nisse had been a widower for three years. He and Ann-Sofie had been happily married, but they never had any children, which had been a source of grief. During summer vacations Embla and her three brothers compensated for that properly. The boys got tired of rural life in their teens but she loved it. Maybe to some degree it was because she got to escape her brothers, but mostly it was because she felt at home with life in the countryside and on the farm.

For a while she had seriously considered becoming a farmer but hesitated because she knew what drudgery the job entailed. The farm could not even support Nisse and Ann-Sofie; he worked at the sawmill and she delivered newspapers.

It was Nisse who suggested that Embla start boxing. He himself had been district champion in his weight class before he got married and took over the farm. Perhaps he had seen that she needed an outlet for all the anxiety she harbored as a teenager, though she hadn't brought it up or told him where the racing thoughts came from.

She had never told anyone about Lollo.

It was also her uncle who had sparked her interest in hunting the summer she turned fifteen. He had asked her if she wanted to go still-hunting; a group planned to shoot some of the mangy foxes that had been seen in the area. Of course Embla thought that sounded really exciting and said yes at once. But it wasn't nearly as thrilling as she had hoped. Sometimes they all stood motionless before someone would suddenly start sneaking carefully in a direction where he thought he saw a movement or heard some rustling. They never saw a trace of any fox, with or without mange.

Despite that uneventful introduction, Embla had become interested, and for the next three years she took part in the drive during the moose hunt. When she turned eighteen she took the hunting test. Since then she and Nisse had hunted together several times a year. Mostly they hunted in the fall, starting in early August when deer and wild boar were in season.

Embla unpacked and hung up her clothes in the minimal wardrobe. There was a shower enclosure in the guest bathroom, but she had showered before she left Gothenburg. A few dabs of deodorant, a couple sprays of perfume, and a nice-looking sweater would have to do. Mascara and lip gloss was more than enough makeup; she would only be meeting with the hunting party.

Nisse was waiting down the hall. Dressed in a fresh white shirt, light-blue knit sweater, light-gray chinos, and new light-gray leather shoes, he looked like he could be on the cover of GQ. Around him was a light air of the aftershave she had given him as a Christmas present the year before.

"How stylish you are! What's her name?" Embla asked happily.

His weathered face took on a shade of polished copper. "Uh . . . or . . . Ingela," he stammered.

"How nice! Ingela Franzén?"

"The pastor's widow! Are you crazy? No, Ingela Gustavsson at the ICA store. You know who she is, don't you?"

It took a moment for Embla to place her. "Light, rather short, a bit younger than you . . ."

"Yes. She is. Although we . . . People talk. You know how it is . . ."

Here stood her retired uncle, hemming and hawing like a shy teenager trying to talk about his first serious infatuation. It was a bit moving but not that strange, considering that he and Ann-Sofie had been together since they were confirmed.

She gave him a big hug. "That's so great!" Smiling, she handed him one of the wine boxes she had brought with her. "Now let's go to the party and charge up before the hunt! Yee-haw!"

They put on their jackets and went out to the stable. There were Nisse's and Ann-Sofie's old bicycles, shining clean and ready to ride. Nisse always got the bicycles in order before the dinner that kicked off the year's moose hunt. He didn't want to have anything to do with drunk driving—not in a car, anyway. But the equivalent on something with handlebars he could overlook.

Because Karin and Björn Bergström had the biggest kitchen, they had been unanimously chosen to host the annual potluck dinner, which they were more than happy to do.

The eight members of the hunting party were gathered around the table, along with the three Bergström children and Einar's and Tobias's wives. Embla knew everyone around the table but one, Peter Hansson. He had recently moved to the area—or perhaps moved *back* was the way to put it—and was the hunting party's newest member.

Embla observed him in secret. She knew that he was thirty-eight years old, but he looked younger. Given his athletic build, it was clear that he worked out. And he was tall and good-looking with blue eyes and rather long, thick blond hair. The thin linen shirt he wore was just casual enough. The collar was unbuttoned and she could see a little gold cross at his throat. When he introduced himself a row of white teeth was exposed in a pleasant smile. *Bleached?* she thought automatically. She also noted the appreciative look she got from him.

She was immediately grateful that she had changed into her nicer sweater. It was cobalt blue with a wide neckline that left one shoulder bare; she was often told the color matched her eyes. Under it she wore a black camisole with thin straps. High up on her right shoulder, her new tattoo was visible: a furious grizzly bear standing on its hind legs, ready to attack. The tattoo was not large, but it was masterfully executed. She'd had it done during a training camp in Miami, and the tattoo artist was one of the best in Florida.

It was Sixten Svensson who pointed out that there were thirteen at the table. "Not a good omen," he muttered, glancing toward Peter Hansson.

Nisse had warned Embla that the Lindbergs, both father and son, had a negative attitude about the newcomer in the hunting party. Evidently Einar Lindberg had been a prospective buyer of Hansgården on his son, Tobias's, behalf. It was a major, unexpected obstacle that Peter did not want to sell and chose to move back in when his dad died. He was just as pigheaded as his father, the Lindbergs thought. They apparently had a sympathizer in Sixten Svensson. He was the leader of the hunt and had rented Peter's dad's hunting ground for many years because his own land holdings were rather modest. It was generally known that he had really wanted to buy the land. When Peter had taken the hunting test and decided to exploit his hunting rights, Sixten's hunting quota became considerably smaller.

As usual the buffet was plentiful and delicious. Karin had made chanterelle quiche, cheese, fresh-baked bread, warm smoked salmon, Dalsland sausage, grilled herb-marinated fillet of pork, tomato salad, and garlic au gratin potatoes. For dessert a crunchy apple cake with vanilla sauce was served. Embla contributed some boxes of wine that had been recommended in *Aftonbladet*'s latest best-of feature. Peter Hansson had brought two cases of strong beer and a whole bottle of O.P. Anderson aquavit, which made the attitude toward him soften a bit.

Embla sat next to Peter when she saw that no one else did and began to chat with him.

"And what do you do?" she asked after introducing herself.

"I own an IT company in Gothenburg. We work with security issues. All companies have problems with security on the Internet," he said.

"How do you manage to live out here? Don't you have to be in the city? I mean, for the customers and personnel."

"I drive down a few times a week. But most of it I can manage from here."

The mood had been lightened by the good food and drink. Everyone was talking and laughing; no one seemed to care about what she and Peter were talking about. With some hesitation she asked the question that the majority around the table was wondering.

"But why did you move back here again?"

Perhaps he would think she was being nosy. In that case, she could blame it on the fact that she was a police officer and had a habit—or bad habit—of interrogating people.

He took his time before answering, and it showed that he carefully weighed what he would say. "My mom died of cancer . . . my partner and I separated. My grandparents died rather close together. And then Dad's death. It was too much. It felt like I had to . . . change my life. Start over," he said quietly.

For once Embla didn't really know what to say. Nisse had mentioned that Peter's sister had run away when she was in her teens, but he didn't know what had happened to her. Before she stopped to think, the question slipped out. "And what about your sister?"

He started and for a moment something flashed in his eyes. It quickly disappeared but she had time to register it. Perhaps it was just irritation at her intrusive questions.

"We haven't had any contact in a long time."

It was clear this was not something he wanted to discuss. Embla stayed silent and considered her next move.

"Although I'm not all alone on the farm," Peter continued. "I have four bulls that will soon go to slaughter. And some chickens and two cats."

"You like animals."

"Yes. Next year I'm going to invest in a good hunting dog. And four new bulls."

Their glasses were refilled and they sang along with a drinking song, had more food, and continued chatting with each other and the others around the table. Peter asked a few questions about her and she answered frankly.

After a while the question came that all new acquaintances asked.

"Where does the name Embla come from? It's a little unusual."

She gave her standard response: "If I say that my older brothers' names are Atle, Frej, and Kolbjörn, perhaps you'll understand."

"So your parents worshiped the old Norse gods, then?"

The question was asked with a wry smile, but she could hear the underlying seriousness.

"No, more like old hippies. But they wanted distinctive names for their kids and absolutely not biblical ones. Embla is the Old Norse counterpart to Eve."

The answer came without her having to think about it, she had recited that litany many times over the years. She never shared how much she hated her name when she was younger. She had gone by Åsa, her middle name, until she started her career as a police officer. Before long some colleague discovered that her given name was Embla and started calling her that. After a while none of her colleagues called her Åsa. These days she thought the name was pretty cool. It had even become popular in recent years, though she hadn't met any other Emblas when she was little.

"Hippies, huh? What do they do?" Peter asked.

"Dad is a retired journalist. He wrote about culture. Mom is an actress. That was how they met. He was going to interview her. Atle is a doctor, Frej is an actor, and Kolbjörn is a sculptor. He makes butt-ugly things in concrete that he sells for astronomical prices."

"Did you say Kolbjörn? Yes, Kolbjörn Nyström is very well-known. And his brother Frej is, too. Although he works in Stockholm, right?"

My goodness; a little culture vulture, Embla thought. But she kept a straight face and answered, "Yes. He lives there with his husband, Viktor."

Peter nodded, the actor and the news anchor on TV4 were a celebrity couple that often appeared in the media. He asked a few more questions about Embla and became noticeably interested when she told him about her work in the mobile unit.

"Västra Götaland County Bureau of Investigation's

mobile unit is a bit unwieldy. Usually we're just called the Unit. Among ourselves we say VGM," she explained.

"So you and two old guys drive around the countryside all over the region and provide support when the local police don't have sufficient resources. Like super cops."

When he put it like that it sounded pretty corny, but that was basically the way it was. She simply nodded and took a sip from her wine glass. Normally she was very careful with alcohol, but at the annual hunting dinner she usually had both an aquavit and a few glasses of wine.

"What made you decide to start hunting?" she asked to change the subject.

"Now I have land with hunting rights, so why not?"

"Have you ever shot any game?"

"Sure. Deer and hares. But not all that many. I've mostly just practiced at the shooting range."

"And you like it?"

"Absolutely. There's an excitement in the hunt that I like. One moment you're enjoying the calm and the next second it's a full adrenaline rush!"

They raised their glasses and toasted to the hunt. Then Sixten Svensson turned his head and fixed his bloodshot eyes on Peter's.

"Fun! Excitement . . . excitement! Hunting is not fun and exciting. It puts food on the table and, damn it, it's been that way since the Stone Age. Now all of a sudden city people come out and want to shoot because it's *fun*! They're dangerous! Can't shoot. Wound the animals and . . . cause trouble," he hissed.

Embla saw a faint redness spread from Peter's neck and creep upward as he met Sixten Svensson's gaze.

Sixten narrowed his eyes and leered at Peter as he

drew his thin lips into a mean smile. "Speaking of hunting. I don't give a damn that you're just as lousy a hunter as your father. Stick to hunting ladies!"

The others around the table started squirming. It was obvious that Sixten was picking a quarrel.

Without looking at Sixten, Peter got up from the table and thanked everyone for a pleasant evening. With an extra thanks to the hosts he disappeared through the door.

"You are a fucking idiot, Sixten! Can't you handle a few drinks without getting unpleasant? And you were actually friends with Peter's dad," Nisse said angrily.

Once Peter had left the others also started to get up. The party atmosphere was ruined. Tobias's wife hadn't had anything to drink during the evening and drove her husband, her father-in-law, and the tipsy Sixten home.

Embla told Nisse that he should bike home ahead of her. She intended to stay awhile to help Karin.

The two cousins drank a little more wine and talked while they cleared away the dirty dishes.

"Peter's sister, what do you know about her?" Embla asked after a while.

"Well, not much. Peter is a few years older than me, and a boy besides, so we never really played together. And then he moved with his mother to Gothenburg. But I remember his sister. Very pretty. Oooooh, how I admired her hair! Super long and blonde. She was going to high school in Åmål when she disappeared."

There was that familiar stab in the gut. "*When she disappeared . . .*"

"How old was Peter when he and his mother moved?" Embla asked, pushing the unpleasant thoughts aside.

Karin frowned and tried to think. "He was in elementary school . . . but what class . . . I don't really remember."

"And his sister had already taken off by then?"

"Yes. She ran away the year before. In the fall or winter. Evidently she had talked about going to Gothenburg and getting a job."

"Nisse mentioned that the dad was an alcoholic and abused the others in the family."

"Yes, I've heard that, too. I think that's why the sister left and then Peter and his mother. They moved in with her parents in Gothenburg. I guess his sister was already there. Although I recall that they looked for her in the forest because she disappeared without a trace after a party."

They rinsed off the dirty dishes, set them in the dishwasher, and started hand washing the big serving plates and casseroles.

"What is his sister's name?"

Karin stood with her hands in the sink. The detergent bubbles made their way up toward her elbows, and she managed to smear a few onto her bangs as she brushed her hair off her forehead.

"What was her name . . . Yes! Camilla! With a C."

"Why haven't I heard about this family before? I've been coming here since I was little and . . ."

"You hadn't even been born yet when the sister disappeared. You and your brothers came here a few years later. By then all that had already been forgotten and replaced with more recent scandals and gossip. It happened at least thirty years ago!"

EMBLA WAS THE last guest to leave Karin and Björn's farm. It was almost one o'clock, but the night was clear with a radiant full moon and an amazing starry sky. It was cold, just below freezing. Fortunately she had remembered to bring both a stocking cap and mittens with her. She started pedaling slowly toward Nisse's farm. Nature was bathing in the magical light from the moon and stars and she enjoyed the silence. A faint breeze blew through the few remaining leaves on the trees, making them rustle. The night air was full of saturated odors of earth, mushrooms, and rotting plants. Autumn smells. The *hoo, hoo, hoo-hoo-hoo-hoo* of a tawny owl cut through the silence. It was an eerie cry. Nisse had taught her to imitate the call by cupping her hands and blowing through slightly separated thumbs.

Out on the fields big bales of silage wrapped in white plastic shimmered. She could see black shadows in the field by the side of the road. Some of them were lying down on the ground and looked like big stones. Nisse's Highland cattle. They looked sweet with their long, golden-brown coats, but their horns invited caution and respect.

On the opposite side of the road the birch forest had

not thinned out and the brush was dense. The glow of the bike lamp was faint, and Embla biked out into the moonlight to better see potholes and bumps in the road.

Suddenly a flash of light danced in the corner of her eye, and some movement caught her attention. Something white was fluttering among the tree trunks. She braked hard and turned her head but only managed to catch a glimpse of a white garment and long, light hair. The moonlight made the hair and dress glisten. It looked as if the apparition was hovering slightly above the ground before it disappeared in the trees.

When the initial surprise passed, Embla set the bicycle down by the side of the road and quickly jumped across the ditch. She started working her way through the brush toward the place where the white figure had disappeared. Even though she was used to moving in rough terrain, it was difficult. Dense thickets let her through only reluctantly, and slippery stones and roots tried to make her fall. With the trees blocking the moonlight, it was almost impossible to see anything ahead of her. She cursed herself for having left her flashlight in the car, instead of keeping it in her jacket pocket as usual.

When she came up to the spot where she had last seen the mysterious apparition, she found herself on a low knoll. It was the slight elevation that had given her the sense that the figure was hovering. The figure had disappeared into a cluster of straight birch trees on top of the hill.

She held her breath and listened. It was quiet, apart from the dry rustling of the leaves. The tawny owl let out another screech in the distance.

It was pointless to try to look for tracks; it would be better to return in daylight.

When she walked back toward the road she perceived faint sounds behind her. Someone was moving carefully between the birches on the hillock. She felt like she was being watched. She jumped on the bicycle and quickly pedaled away.

NISSE HAD MADE strong coffee for himself and prepared a hearty breakfast of boiled eggs and homemade bread with various toppings. He was well aware of his niece's strict eating habits and had stocked up on natural yogurt, coarse flatbread, soft whole-grain bread, and low-fat cheese. Embla always brought unsweetened muesli and herbal tea with her, plus some mysterious containers of dietary supplements. "Just natural herbs, protein, and minerals. No anabolic steroids," she always reassured him when he suspiciously tried to read the fine print on the labels.

Over breakfast she told him about her peculiar experience on the way home.

"How much did you have to drink?" he said with a teasing smile.

"More than usual. I wasn't stone-cold sober, but I definitely wasn't drunk either. I saw what I saw. And I heard someone moving around in the trees. I want to check on it."

"I see. If you say so . . ."

Resolute, she met his questioning gaze. Neither of them said anything for a long time.

"Okay. We'll go there after we finish eating," he finally said with a sigh.

Embla had problems finding the place where she had gone into the forest to follow after the "Lady in White," as Nisse persisted in calling the nocturnal apparition. After searching for a while she found marks in the grass by the side of the road where she had put down the bike.

"Yep. Here it is."

Without hesitation she went into the thicket on the other side of the road. Because she had forced her way through the vegetation like a bulldozer, all she had to do was follow the broken or damaged branches and look for where the frost-bitten grass had been disturbed.

When they approached the hill, she asked Nisse to wait while she went up. The top was level, like a little plateau. The young birches the white-clad figure had disappeared into were off to the side. Embla started eyeballing the rough grass and hair moss that covered the ground. In some places it was clear the moss had been trampled.

"Nisse! Come here!" she called.

Without saying anything she pointed at the marks. He got down on his knees to take a careful look.

"Yes, someone has been walking here, but you can't see the size of the shoe. Or if it's even a person."

"Okay. But in any case it is evident that someone actually was here last night and that I didn't have acute delirium." She took a few pictures of the marks in the moss with her phone and started carefully inspecting the branches of the birch trees. After a while she found what she was looking for. "Yes!" she said, pointing triumphantly at her find.

A long, light strand of hair was hanging at the very tip

of a thin branch, glistening in the sunlight. Carefully she gathered the strand with the tweezers from her toiletry kit and put it into an ordinary plastic bag that she remembered to bring from Nisse's kitchen.

When they got in the car her phone rang, and she saw on the display that it was Elliot. Before she could say anything his excited voice trumpeted, "Have you got a moose?"

"No, we haven't gone up to the cabin yet. The hunt doesn't start until tomorrow."

"But then you're going to shoot one?"

"Hope so. You know that it goes on for several days."

"I know. Next year I want to come with you!"

She had explained to him at least a thousand times that he had to be fifteen years old to participate. Her hope was that he would lose interest in hunting by then. The boy had no hunting tradition in his family. The mere thought of his father, Jason, patiently sitting on watch for hours in the rain and cold was laughable. During his childhood in Jamaica he had never heard about either Sweden or moose, and that hadn't really changed during his youthful years in Miami either. But Embla answered the same way she always did.

"When you've turned fifteen. You have to be at least that old to join in."

"Do you have to?"

The disappointment in his voice sounded equally genuine every time. If you've just turned eight it feels like an eternity to fifteen.

She asked how he was doing with her cousins. Sulkily he let it be known that he would much rather have stayed with her hunting party in the forest. *Manipulative like his dad*, she thought. It had been several years since she and Jason had separated, but the bond between Embla and his son had become strong during the year they lived together. Jason was a well-known saxophonist and often had to travel for engagements. When she could she was more than happy to take care of the boy. This week Jason was at a jazz festival in Stockholm, and because she would be hunting, Elliot had to stay with her aunt's family. He had no memories of his mother because she died when he was not quite a year old. Perhaps that made it easier for him and Embla to connect. Although the strongest reason was probably that they simply enjoyed being together. But she had noticed he was starting to become more and more like his father. The darned kid always managed to guide the conversation to how she had betrayed him and made his dad drop him off with her aunt.

"I miss you," Elliott said in a low voice. "It's no fun when you're not here."

It took her a moment before she could answer. "I miss you too. Hugs," she said a little thickly.

When she ended the call they sat quietly a moment.

"What do you think about bringing the kid up here during fall break? A few days or so," Nisse proposed at last.

"He would love that!"

She would tell Elliot that the next time they spoke—he would start the countdown immediately.

AFTER LUNCH THEY stopped by the mailbox outside the ICA store. Embla had a letter she wanted to send. It was addressed to her boss, Superintendent Göran

Krantz at VGM and contained the long strand of hair, along with a handwritten note that asked him to analyze it. As a reason for her inquiry she simply wrote: *I'll explain when I know more.*

From there, they continued over to Karin and Björn's farm. Everyone in the hunting party parked their cars on the farmyard and rode over together in two bigger cars. The last five kilometers up to the cabins they had to drive on a logging road that wound through the forest. Calling it a road was an exaggeration, it was just wheel tracks from logging machinery. Only four-wheel-drive vehicles could advance on that miserable surface.

This year there was a third car that could manage the logging road. Peter Hansson was driving a new Range Rover. The paint was metallic dark blue and the chrome glistened. *Good-looking and expensive*, thought Embla. She and Nisse moved their baggage, which also included Seppo, over to Björn's Jeep. If more stowage room was needed there was also a brand-new Nissan Navara SE that Einar and Tobias owned. Sixten and Tilly were also riding in their big pickup. The latter was a female Drever, a very capable hunting dog that was starting to get a bit up in years.

The men at Dalsnäs Manor were also getting ready to depart. The estate manager, Stig Ekström, was driving a late-model, red King Cab, and his Hamilton foxhound was along for the ride. According to his fine pedigree, his name was "Freival's Diamond's Pathfinder," but no one cared about that. He answered to the name of Frippe. Anders von Beehn owned the dog, but it was the Ekströms who took care of it between hunts and attended to training and practice sessions.

Stig Ekström was also responsible for transporting the day's catch to the butchering shed and helping the others hang the gutted carcasses on sturdy hooks from the ceiling. Stig was also in the habit of bringing the hunters dinner that his wife, Anna, had prepared the day before, and she was a talented cook.

That morning, all five hunters rode in the Hummer. Anders drove the heavy vehicle while he talked to his hunting comrades. The conversation was conducted in English for Volker's sake, which was no problem for Anders, who had lived in both England and the US and spoke the language fluently.

"I should explain how the hunt here is organized. Since my great-grandfather's time, Dalsnäs has been one of the owners of the hunting grounds on the border between Norway and the Swedish provinces of Dalsland and Värmland. There are five other hunting rights holders in the area. The ancestors of these farmers and landowners got the forestland as payment for a big gravel pit and a peat bog. At that time the forest was considered rather worthless. Much later my great-grandfather managed to buy up over seven thousand acres of forest, but unfortunately it was from different landowners, which is why our hunting ground today is not clearly demarcated or even contiguous. The other landowners' combined acreage is almost exactly the same size as the portion I inherited. So for practical reasons, we've run the hunt together since my great-grandfather's time—so we're talking somewhere in the late eighteen hundreds. We hunt under a joint leader and divide the game fairly. The advantage is that we have a good allotment of game."

"Do we socialize with the others in the evenings?" Volker asked.

"Not usually. The other group has their own hunting cabins a few hundred meters from mine. But those men are capable hunters. And the women, too, for that matter."

"The women?" the German said, raising his eyebrows.

"Yes, two of them. They've participated for several years."

THE THREE THATCHED-ROOF cabins were placed in a U formation in a large clearing. They parked the cars on the yard between the cabins and started unpacking. Nisse, Embla, and the Bergströms would stay in the biggest cabin. Nisse and his father had built the cabin when the old one was too run-down. It consisted of three small bedrooms with a bunk bed in each and a rather modest living room. In one corner of the living room there was a kitchenette with both a refrigerator and a stove, run on butane. The furniture consisted of a big gateleg table and eight old spindle-backed chairs.

Einar and Tobias Lindberg stayed in the adjoining cabin. It only had two bedrooms and because it did not have a living room, they always went over to Nisse's. The same was true of Sixten Svensson, whose cabin was a somewhat more dilapidated version of Lindberg's. This year he would stay there with Peter Hansson. Technically, the cabin belonged to Peter; it was his land and hunting right. Sixten's land area was considerably smaller, and he had never had a cabin of his own. When he had rented the land from Peter's father, he stayed alone in the cabin. The two men were childhood friends and happily shared a bottle, but Sixten had always called the old man "the bloodsucker" to the rest of the group, even though the rent was low. And now he had to try to get along with Hansson's son.

A newly constructed outhouse stood a short distance from the cabins. It was built over a deep hole and supplied with plentiful quantities of carbolic lime to help prevent odor and keep insects and animals away. The lime sack was in a small plastic barrel with a cover on the bench beside the seat. When the hunting party had its annual cleaning day at the end of August, the task of tidying the outhouse had fallen to Embla. After checking on the lime level in the small plastic barrel beside the seat, she had replenished the toilet paper rolls. To finish it off she placed a bundle of *Hunting Ground* magazines on the small stool that was inside the outhouse.

Planning for the hunt would start at three o'clock sharp; the hunting leader, Sixten Svensson, was particular about that. As usual it would be held at von Beehn's. Even though his hunting cabin was built of timber, it was an understatement to call it a cabin. The building was considerably bigger than Nisse's farmhouse. They usually called it the Hunting Castle. It was built on a hill above a small, unnamed lake. If you wanted to swim you had to take the trouble to go down a steep slope to access the small beach—not that it was ever warm enough to swim during the week of the hunt. Behind the Hunting Castle Anders had had a glass veranda constructed with a view of the water. A few meters from the veranda, the hill dropped ten meters right to the water. Given the gentlemen's habit of relieving their bladders after a few beers over the edge of the drop, it was called, a bit irreverently, the "Piss-ipice." To prevent anyone from getting too close to the edge after the onset of darkness, a light post had been mounted a few steps from the drop.

In the early 1960s Anders von Beehn's father had already made sure to have electricity brought in, which had cost a tidy sum. The house also had running water from a separately drilled well but no toilet because that would require a tank for the drainage. But there were facilities for both laundry and showering, as well as a good-sized sauna.

Every year when Embla came into the big room she had a feeling that she had been transported a hundred years back in time. The house was built early in the previous century, and the furnishings in the main room had been untouched since then. The big, open fireplace was made of granite blocks. The hearth was high enough that a man of normal height could stand upright in it, and whole logs were burned, not some trifling little blocks of wood. Several stately moose horns hung on the chimney. The walls had high wainscoting. Above them an artist had depicted the Norse gods and other motifs from ancient Nordic mythology, but strikingly, a number of the figures were bare-breasted Valkyries and athletic Vikings drinking mead out of large horns. Even though the colors had faded over the years, the paintings were still impressive. In the hall there were two long tables with enough chairs that everyone could have a seat. By tradition Anders treated everyone to coffee and cinnamon rolls.

Because they had a foreign guest, Anders translated the hunting leader's instructions. For Volker's and Peter Hansson's sakes Sixten Svensson started by explaining where all the game crossings and paths went. Like the conscientious hunting leader he was, he had marked on a map where the stands were, and he had also numbered them all. The stands would be cleaned out during the afternoon so they would have clear fields of fire. It was just a matter of "taking a brush cutter and mowing down the shit," as Sixten had said.

With a gloomy expression he reported that the year's hunting quota had been reduced by one adult moose and a calf.

"But that was probably to be expected with all the wolf-lovers in Stockholm who make the decisions. For that reason we only get to shoot fourteen adults and fifteen calves this year," he said bitterly.

Sixten pointed out the stands on the map while he informed the participants what number they had. For the most part they kept the same numbers year after year, but sometimes someone wanted to change, which was no problem since there were several extra stands.

He showed which firing directions were prohibited and told the group he had marked them with red plastic markers.

"And don't forget the red band on your hat!" With that final remark he thanked them for their attention and asked if anyone had any questions.

Peter raised his hand. "I'd like a different stand," he said.

Sixten swallowed hard several times, and his Adam's apple bobbed up and down on his skinny neck. Peter did not look away.

"The one on the back side of the hill is available. And it's on my land," he said.

Sixten swallowed several more times before he managed to force out, "I see. Well . . . then you can have it."

Peter hadn't sounded perturbed, but Embla saw how his eyes had narrowed as he was speaking. *Those two truly despise each other*, she thought. How had Peter known that he'd gotten a bad stand? What Sixten had allotted him was on the edge of a bog and everyone in the hunting party knew animals seldom passed there. Peter must have inspected his land and his cabin, which made some sense since he was a new landowner and hunting rights holder.

During the run-through Sixten had not said anything about which stand he himself intended to claim and could therefore pretend he hadn't been aiming for what Peter wanted. He pointed at the map. "I'll take number fourteen."

That was one of two stands that did not have complete backstop in all directions, but those who had been on previous hunts knew that it was a good spot where game often passed by.

"And because I'll be sitting there, I will naturally be extra careful about checking the markers," Sixten continued, managing to purse his lips into a strained smile.

Everyone chuckled at the joke and the slightly tense atmosphere loosened up. They stood up and thanked Anders for the coffee. Now it was a matter of clearing up the stands and the stand lines while there was still daylight.

AS DARKNESS FELL the preparations began for the first dinner of the hunting days. In keeping with tradition, they had a rich moose stew the evening before the hunt. As usual Karin made the stew with a lot of mushrooms, onions, thyme, red wine, and cream. Nisse and Embla provided the meat; they always saved at least two kilos of last year's stew pieces in his big freezer. Einar and Tobias relaxed; they were responsible for the next day's grilling. As expected Sixten contributed a case of strong beer. There was also wine for anyone who preferred that, and Karin had remembered to bring along the leftover wine boxes from the potluck. To Embla's irritation Peter pulled out a fresh bottle of O.P. Anderson, and he had remembered to bring small plastic drinking glasses to go with it.

The good food, beer, and aquavit lightened up the atmosphere around the table. Embla observed their new hunting companion in secret. Peter did not say very much, but he smiled amiably and poured shots for whoever wanted some. He looked just as handsome in the red-checked flannel shirt as he had in the white linen. A small gold cross glistened at his throat. From what she could see, he did not have more than one shot of aquavit himself. *Handsome and pleasant but wants to stay in control*, she thought. And after Sixten's attack over dinner—not to mention the peevish air between them during the hunt meeting that afternoon—she could understand why. The two of them would also be sharing a cabin: another reason to maintain a clear head.

EMBLA'S CELL PHONE gave a cheerful tune at five-thirty. Half asleep, she reached for it on the nightstand but woke up completely as she fumbled in empty air. She realized that she was in the hunting cabin and that the phone was on the floor. Yawning, she leaned down to turn off the alarm, stretched, and then got out of the narrow bed, deftly managing to avoid hitting her head on the top bunk.

She quickly got dressed, found the flashlight, and went out to the privy. It was still dark. The full moon was hidden behind thick clouds. A faint breeze passed through the treetops, and she felt the cold lightly scratching against her cheeks and biting the end of her nose.

When she came in again, the aroma of coffee filled the cabin. Nisse was making coffee for everyone in the hunting party in a big aluminum pot.

Embla and Karin helped set the table. Due to the early morning hour they did not exchange many words; once they had a little breakfast in them they usually got more talkative. Each person in the party had to make their own sandwiches to take into the forest. Likewise everyone filled their thermoses; it was important to stay warm all day.

Einar and Tobias came in with a tired, stiff Tilly. The dog collapsed on the floor next to the stove and fell back asleep at once. She would perk up as soon as they were out in the woods.

The next moment Peter stepped through the door with a friendly "good morning." Sixten arrived last and grunted as usual at everyone and no one in particular.

It was chilly in the cabin but because they had their hunting clothes on, no one felt cold. Embla always thought she looked like one of the guys. On a scale of one-to-ten her glamour factor was zero. She had put on a light-gray wool sweater with a short zipper in the high collar, and under that she wore a long-sleeved flannel shirt layered on top of a T-shirt. Her jacket and pants were of a flexible water- and wind-proof material. Her boots were sturdy and practical. And the hunting cap that completed the finery was a bright red-orange.

Before they left the cabin she retrieved the most important thing: the rifle, a 6.5 caliber Sako. And she remembered to take a box of ammunition. Last year she had forgotten that and had to go back to the cabin to retrieve the bullets.

A FAINT DAWN crept from the east as she settled in on the tower. To Embla, this was the best time of the whole hunt. The darkness was just starting to let up, there was a stillness in the air, and she had a heightened awareness of all the scents surrounding her. As she sat there in the stand, she was aware of the watchfulness inside her. At dawn and twilight the wild animals are usually moving, and that was the best time to catch sight of them.

But around her stand it seemed calm that clear morning.

The only living being that disturbed the peace was a boreal owl that landed in a pine tree not far from her. It was a breed that was rarely seen, but the little owl looked at her unafraid, its big yellow eyes glistening in the semi-darkness, giving it an almost demonic appearance. After a minute or so it flew off with jerky wing strokes but then quickly rose in circles over the clearing a short distance away.

As the upper part of the sun's disk started to appear over the spruce tops, a light gust of wind made the remaining leaves on the aspen trees tremble and rustle. Like so often before the start of the hunt, she thought she sensed a streak of sorrow in the wind as it passed through the treetops. Many of the forest's inhabitants would die during the next few weeks. At the same time she was convinced that hunting was necessary; the population of game must be kept at a certain level to prevent damage to the forest and collisions on the roads.

The sound of a shot broke the silence, and her adrenaline came rushing. The feeling was always the same when the first shot went off. Now the hunt has started! A few minutes later Sixten's voice crackled over the two-way radio.

"Break! Search for wounded moose cow. The search will be between stands three, five, six, and seven. Will come back when I know more about which direction the animal is moving. Over and out!"

Shit! The hunt had barely begun before someone messed things up, Of course, it could happen to the best; the animal could jump and change direction. But Embla was irritated that the year's hunt started with a wounded animal.

After half an hour of searching the dogs caught up with the moose cow. They were barking excitedly. The cow had been hit in the front leg, a good ways down on the shoulder. *Clumsy!* thought Embla, pursing her lips in her solitude up in the tower. Nisse would bring down the wounded animal.

AT NOON SIXTEN'S voice was heard again on the two-way radio: "Gathering at the meeting place."

The temperature had risen to a few degrees above freezing, and the sunshine flooded down between the branches of the trees. A squirrel scampered up and down a tree trunk. Curiously it looked at Embla with its sprightly eyes from a safe position behind the trunk. She stopped and clicked her tongue at it. It didn't let itself be lured, and disappeared up to the crown of the tree instead.

The meeting place was a clearing where the hunting party had buried a large cement pipe in the ground. Half an hour earlier someone had filled the pipe with wood and lit it. The fire had died down to perfect grilling embers. Around the grill there were rough logs to sit on. Most preferred to stand; you got stiff after sitting at the station for several hours. Einar and Tobias placed a loose grate over the cement pipe and spread out sausages of various lengths and sizes on the makeshift grill. Beside them were some bags of buns and magnum bottles of ketchup and mustard. The aroma from the sausages made Embla's stomach contract with hunger.

She went over and set her cleared rifle with the others' guns. At the same moment she caught sight of von Beehn's hunting party, who came walking through the bushes. The Swedes in his group had Carl Gustafs, caliber 30-06, but the new guy who had joined von Beehn and the others—German, she figured, based on his accent—had a rifle that she thought looked like a Heym. A beautiful shotgun. She turned her eyes away when she discovered that the German was inspecting her. Reflexively she brought her hand up toward her eyebrow. She had removed the surgical tape from the championship match some time ago, but a light swelling and discoloration were still there.

That dork Greger Liljon had dressed in a tweed jacket, golf pants, knee socks, expensive boots, and cap. She knew he was the nephew of Anders von Beehn. He had been there during the last three hunts, but they had never spoken. *An out-and-out upper-class brat*, she had thought the first time she saw him. That impression had remained.

"He's the one who wounded the moose cow," Karin whispered in her ear. The cousins exchanged a meaningful look.

Sixten began to speak and declared himself satisfied with the morning. They had killed two yearling calves and two adult moose cows, including the wounded cow.

Anders said that at about ten o'clock Greger had caught sight of a stately sixteen-pointer, but he didn't have a good firing angle. He gave his nephew a sharp look, who blushed and tried to pretend he didn't detect the gibe, but his wandering gaze betrayed him.

Embla saw that he seemed ill at ease. He continuously rubbed his palms against his wool pants and rocked worriedly in his expensive boots. His whole body language signaled how tense he was.

The dogs sat among the hunters and begged for pieces of sausage here and there. Happiness for them came when someone fumbled a bun and dropped a sausage on the ground.

Sixten stuck strictly to the prohibition on alcohol

during the hunt itself, but Embla wondered to herself whether Jan-Eric had broken the agreement. His face was ruddy, he laughed too loud, and when he took his sausage and bun it was obvious his hands were shaking.

The last one to arrive was Peter Hansson. He looked energetic and fresh and declared that he was starving. When Embla asked how he thought his first morning as a moose hunter had been, he answered happily, "Uneventful but completely amazing!" He hadn't seen any moose, but, he said with a grin, he had seen several deer and a badger.

The day before Sixten had informed them that they were right next to a wolf preserve with a parent couple and at least two cubs. Besides that, a bear—a female with a cub—had been spotted in the vicinity late in the summer. There was even pictorial evidence. The pictures were somewhat blurry because the woman out picking cloudberries had shivered as she took a picture with her phone. Fortunately the bear took no notice of her; there had been a pretty good distance between them.

Peter said that he hoped to catch sight of at least one of the predators that were in the area. *Good luck,* thought Embla. The older men in the party had hunted for forty years or more and had only encountered a wolf on scattered occasions. Embla had never seen one herself. Sixten claimed to have met wolves at least twenty times, but he was alone in that, and there was a question about whether his claim was true. The only real close contact with predators that any of them had had was when Einar walked right into a bear during the moose hunt six years ago. Fortunately the bear only glared at him, then turned around and lumbered off. What saved him that time was that he didn't have Tilly with him.

THREE ADULT ANIMALS and five yearling calves. That was a good result for the first day's hunt, Sixten summarized contentedly.

It had taken time to prepare the animals and hang the carcasses up in the shed. It was almost eight o'clock before everyone was gathered around the table in the bigger cabin. On the yard outside Tobias and Einar were grilling grouse, so according to Sixten it "stank like a fucking crematorium." But the Lindbergs were true grill masters and had brought a bottle of their homemade secret-recipe oil with them up to the cabins. Sixten, Einar, and Tobias had shot the grouse during a few days of hunting at the end of August. The birds had been carefully prepared, boiled, and frozen ahead of the moose hunt.

Powdered béarnaise sauce would have to do, which Nisse whipped up in a saucepan on the stove. Karin conjured up a large bowl of potato salad, and with the last tomatoes from Björn's greenhouse at home on the farm, it was a real feast.

With the food they had water, beer, or wine. Once again Peter hauled out a bottle of O.P. Anderson and new small plastic shot glasses. *Why must he treat to aquavit every evening?* Embla thought. The others could usually stop after one or two shots, but Sixten drank until the bottle was empty.

When Nisse put on the coffee kettle after dinner, Sixten said suddenly, "I wonder what's gotten into Frippe."

"What do you mean?" Nisse asked.

"Don't know. Stig said the dog seemed out of sorts. It was lying in the car and looked sick. It vomited. Couldn't even raise its head. I think Stig should take the dog straight to the vet. I know it's getting a bit late, but the one in Ed has a home practice, so he promised to take a look at the dog."

Einar frowned and sent a worried glance toward Tilly, who was sleeping on a patch of rug in front of the stove. She was the same as always but the others understood his worry. It could be something contagious.

Nisse looked at Seppo, who was lying on the wood floor next to his friend. When the dog felt his master's gaze, he raised his head at once and stood up. *Are we going out? Yes, yes! Please!* his whole body language said. He too was the same as usual, alert and sensitive to signals.

"I'm going out for a walk with Seppo. Tilly can come along if she wants," said Embla.

"I'll join you and hold the flashlight," Peter said quickly.

Tobias's expression turned dark but he could hardly say anything. Married with two children, he forced himself to keep quiet. The summer vacation when they were fourteen he and Embla had had a summer flirtation, and it was as if he had never completely let it go.

"Embla, watch out if he asks you to hold the flashlight. You may get something else altogether in your hand!" he threw out after them.

"All the same. Just so it shines!" she responded.

It was nice to get out, the air inside the cabin got heavy after a while. Thick clouds concealed the moon and the darkness was impenetrable. She was grateful that Peter had offered to go along; it would have been hard to manage two dogs on leashes while holding a flashlight, and she didn't dare let them run around on their own. There were predators in the vicinity; the butchering offal that was left behind in the woods after the day's hunt lured them out.

Peter turned on the flashlight and they started walking across the yard. After a short silence he asked, "Does von Beehn have another dog?"

"No. His dad always had several, but Anders only has one."

"Then the gang in the Hunting Castle won't have a dog tomorrow."

"No. It's a shame because Frippe is really good, but there are these two dogs, too." She was forced to stop to untangle the leashes, which had gotten twisted up during Seppo's meandering.

"I can take one of them," Peter offered.

"Thanks."

They walked a bit in silence. The beam of light played across the ground, revealing branches and hollows that could treacherously fell a hiker.

Now or never, she thought. "Listen . . . I have to ask you something."

"Yes?"

"Why do you always treat everyone to aquavit?"

"What do you mean? I thought that was part of it."

The surprise in his voice sounded genuine.

"Maybe in the past. But we're trying to skip strong alcohol during the hunt for Sixten's sake. As you know, he gets worked up once he starts drinking."

"Sure, I know. But I actually brought the bottles with him in mind. To be honest, I was hoping it would make him like me better."

"Is the fuss about the rent?"

He sighed audibly. "Yes. He wanted to buy Dad's land. Obviously at a low price. When I didn't agree to that, he proposed renting it all. But I said no because I wanted to start hunting myself. He got really upset."

"He is a little . . . special."

"Yes, I've realized that. I said that of course he could keep a room in the cabin, but I don't know if that made things any better."

Feuds between neighbors over land can get terribly contentious, she knew from her time in the mobile unit. Land was the only resource there can never be more of. *The earth that exists is all that we have and that's what we have to fight about*, as Nisse liked to say.

They walked awhile without speaking. There was rustling from small animals in the undergrowth. A bird suddenly shrieked shrilly very close by. Both of them started and the dogs barked.

"That sounded like a soul in distress," she said, to dismiss her fear.

Peter did not answer but quickened his pace. When he realized that she had a hard time seeing where to put her feet, he stopped and waited. She noticed that his breathing sounded a bit fast. Presumably he was still not used to all the sounds of the forest and had gotten scared. Side by side they walked in the direction of the outhouse; the path could only faintly be made out in the light. At last he broke the silence.

"How long are you and Nisse staying up here?"

"Until Thursday evening. It's usually just Nisse, me, and Sixten by the time Thursday rolls around. The others work and leave on Wednesday. But they'll come up here again over the weekend and we will, too. Then we hunt all day Saturday and half of Sunday. On Sunday afternoon we start cutting up what we've killed during these first three hunting days."

Peter was silent for a long time. "And von Beehn's group? Do they stay?" he asked at last.

"Just Anders and Jan-Eric. They always go home on Sunday. Ola Forsnaess did, too, but as you know he was killed in a car accident after the last moose hunt. So this year it might just be Anders and Jan-Eric. The others will probably go home on Wednesday."

They continued up to the outhouse in silence. When they were there Peter cleared his throat. "If you want to go in I can hold the dogs . . ."

"I don't need to. Karin and I usually go right before bedtime. It can feel a little eerie to walk alone in the dark with the wolves and other predators around." She couldn't see his face but sensed that he smiled in the darkness.

"If you have time you can come and visit and see what things are like at the farm," he said.

His comment had come completely by surprise, and she didn't know how to respond. *Was it an invitation for something more?* she thought, before rejecting the idea. No, he was probably just being friendly, and he may be a little lonely. Embla was aware that she was feeling more and more interest in the man who was walking beside her. She knew that she always fell for the wrong guys: the slightly unreliable and dangerous ones, the ones who didn't need her and that she definitely didn't need. But Peter didn't fit into her usual pattern. He gave signals that he was available, and he seemed rather harmless with his computers, the farm, and the animals. And he looked good. *A real hottie!* as her friend Mia always said.

"I'll have to see if I have time on Friday," she answered in a suitably nonchalant tone.

"Well, then I have to drive down to Gothenburg. I've got a new major customer in the works, and we're going out for dinner afterward. But I'll try to come back up here on Saturday. So maybe next week or the following weekend?"

"Maybe. I have vacation then, too." To her own surprise she felt disappointed. Friday would have suited her just fine. But he did have a company to run.

In silence they walked back toward the cabin.

The others were just getting up from the table. Tobias gave them a searching look but didn't say anything.

"Shall we?" Karin whispered in her ear.

"We shall."

They took a flashlight and went out in the darkness. A dozen meters from the cabin they stopped and went behind some juniper bushes where they crouched and peed. They did that sometimes in the evenings when they didn't feel like going all the way over to the outhouse.

When Embla sank down on her hard bed she set the alarm on her phone for five-thirty. Carefully she placed her iPhone on the floor. Like so many times before, she thought she ought to arrange a stool or a chair beside the bed but was too lazy to get up and do it.

SHE WAS AWAKENED by a frightful noise. It took a few seconds before she realized that it was the alarm on the phone, working its way up to highest volume. Half asleep, she fumbled for the phone, which had slid under the bed, and managed to silence it. Exhausted from the effort she fell back against the pillow. The little bedroom was freezing and her nose felt ice cold, but inside the thick sleeping bag it was wonderfully warm and cozy. She longed to stay in bed for one more hour, especially given the weather. She could hear rain pattering against the windowpane. Or was it snow? It was a bit early in the season, but it was not at all impossible. The hunting area was high up, where it was always a lot colder than it was down on the flatlands. A few years ago they had had to plod to their stations in inch-deep snow. It was tough but with the right clothing and footwear it hadn't been a problem.

No, now you have to get up! she urged herself. If she lay there any longer there was a major risk that she would fall back asleep. Listlessly she started stretching in her lovely cocoon, when she suddenly stopped. What was that? She listened tensely to try to make out the sound again. There. It was definitely a scream. And another. It sounded like a woman. Karin! She wriggled herself free from the sleeping bag and leaped out of bed. In her haste she struck her head on the top bunk but barely noticed it. The room was completely dark but she knew where on the wall the hooks she had hung her clothes on were. At a furious speed she got dressed. She slept in her long underwear and socks, so it was just a matter of pulling on her sweater and jumping into the pants.

At the front door Nisse was already stepping into his boots. Without exchanging a word with him she pulled on her boots and rushed out into the rain, wriggling into her jacket. While doing that she managed to fish out the flashlight that was in the pocket. For a fraction of a second she stopped to turn it on and try to establish where the scream had come from. The outhouse. Definitely the outhouse. She aimed the beam of light toward the almost-invisible path and ran as fast as she could. Ahead of her she saw Björn. He hadn't had time to put on his jacket and was running in just a flannel shirt that was sticking damply to his back.

The beams of the flashlights showed where Karin was leaning against the door, sobbing loudly.

"Karin! What is it?" Björn ran up and threw his arms around her.

At first she couldn't answer but when he carefully tried to move her from the door she got a wild look in her eyes and resisted with all her strength. "No, don't open it!" she screamed.

"Why not?"

"A snake . . . it bit me!"

"A snake?" Embla and Björn echoed.

Behind them steps from the others were heard approaching.

When he recovered from the initial surprise Björn asked, "Where did it bite you?"

"Here . . . on my hand. I was going to get toilet paper . . . it was by the roll."

She held out her right hand. In the sharp light from the flashlights two distinct red dots were visible right below her little finger. The bite was deep, and it was clear she needed to see a doctor.

"There's poor cell phone coverage here. I'll drive her and contact the health center on the way," said Björn.

"I can drive you both in my car if you'd like," Peter offered.

"No, thanks. It's just as well we take the Jeep. You have two cars left here so you can get home. It's best that you continue the hunt. I'll be in touch."

He put his arm around Karin to support her. In silence the others in the hunting party watched as the light from their flashlights got weaker and weaker as Karin and Björn headed back toward the cabins.

"And what do we do with the snake?" Tobias said in the darkness.

"I have a spade in the car," his father said sternly.

"Vipers are protected," Peter added carefully.

"Not here," Einar cut him short.

They cracked open the door of the outhouse and the flashlights lit up the small space.

The black snake was coiled up on the stool, above the pile of magazines. Its head was raised a few centimeters and its tongue played out and in. Its movements were slow because of the cold, but it did not look amiably inclined. It hissed at them through its open jaws.

"A female. They're bigger than the males. And the rump is rounder," Sixten informed them.

"So it's not a grass snake?" Peter asked.

"No, it doesn't have spots on the side of its head. Although they don't always have those."

With long steps, Einar came walking through the rain. In one hand he was holding the spade. Without further ado he opened the door completely, raised the spade, and chopped down with the sharp edge against the snake. There was such force in the blow that the creature's head bounced away and landed right by the door, and the first few magazines in the pile were split down the middle.

They helped to get Karin's and Björn's things in the car; it was unclear whether they would be able to come back up for the weekend. While they were packing up, the swelling on Karin's hand and fingers had increased. It hurt, she admitted, but she seemed to have recovered from the initial shock.

Being bitten by a viper in the middle of October was unusual; no one in the hunting party had heard of any other cases this late in the season. Snakes usually get sluggish and are dormant when the temperature drops toward freezing. This specimen had seemed rather active. *And how in the world did it get in?* Embla wondered.

Almost twenty years ago Nisse had put heavy metal sheets wherever mice might try to make their way into the cabin, and he had done the same with the outhouse. The sheets were impossible for rats and mice to get through, and they hadn't had any problems with rodents since then. The only possibility was that the snake had slithered down into the latrine pit and come up by way of the lavatory opening. But that explanation wasn't likely because no trace of carbolic lime could be seen on the headless body. Besides, a heavy wooden lid covered the hole, and the snake hardly could have moved it and certainly couldn't have closed it again.

At ten o'clock a text message came from Björn, who wrote to say the doctor at the community health center had given Karin a shot of cortisone. She was up-to-date on her tetanus shot because she worked in healthcare. Now she had been given strict orders to take it easy for a few days. For the moment, Björn said, he had lost the desire to hunt, but maybe he would drive up to the cabin on Saturday.

THREATENING CLOUDS ROLLED across the sky all morning and when it was time for group grilling it started to rain.

Most of the hunters stood by the fire, waiting for sausage. As Peter walked by, Sixten raised his voice and said, "A sick dog and a hunter bitten by a snake. That has never happened before. Remember what I said about thirteen at the table!"

Peter ignored him and went up to Embla, who had just set her rifle down against a tree. He nodded toward the rifle. "Doesn't that have a pretty strong recoil?" he asked.

She could have informed him that she was probably the one in the hunting party who could best handle recoil, given her training on guns and the strong musculature in her neck and shoulders, but she didn't.

"Yeah, but you acquire the technique. Although to start with, I had a lighter rifle that's suitable for a moving hunt. The recoil is considerably less," she answered instead.

"Because I'm such a greenhorn I really feel the shock. But I guess you learn."

"You do," she said, smiling encouragingly.

"Okay. Can you show me how to position the butt so I don't feel it as much?" After a moment, Peter blushed at the innuendo.

"Sure," Embla said with a smile.

She picked up his new Blaser R8 caliber 9.3x62 and felt its weight. It was an excellent all-around gun, but she could understand why he had problems with the rifle's strong recoil. They moved a short distance away from their hunting comrades at the grill and stood with their backs to them. In front of them were only spruce trees and brush. He took a sight out of his jacket pocket and mounted it on the rifle. It was a smaller Zeiss. She used a similar one herself when she didn't need her red-dot sight.

"Show me how you hold the gun when you aim," she said.

He got into shooting position. They were standing very close to each other, so she could study his profile without it seeming intrusive. Straight nose, blue eyes that were shadowed by dense, light eyelashes. Peter was good-looking. Really good-looking.

She adjusted the location of the butt plate and raised it somewhat. "There. Feel it properly. That's the best position to resist the recoil," she said.

"Like this?"

"Yep." She watched as he got a feel for the position.

"And here you are, necking!"

The voice behind them made them both jump. Peter turned around, still with the rifle in shooting position. It happened to be aimed at a point right above the bridge of Tobias's nose. His eyes widened and the smile on his lips disappeared. Embla threw herself against the barrel and took hold of it with both hands. With all her strength she aimed it down toward the ground.

"Never do that again, damn it!" she roared.

With flushed cheeks she yanked the rifle from his hands and for a moment it looked as if she intended to throw it into the bushes, but she stopped herself and without a word she threw the sporting rifle back to its owner. Luckily Peter managed to catch the gun. The two men stood crestfallen and watched her straight back as she marched off, seething with anger. Both were unsure which of them she was most angry at.

The truth was she didn't know herself. She was literally shaking with fury. It was so idiotic of Tobias to surprise a person who was standing in shooting position and completely dangerous of Peter to react the way he did. Never aiming your gun at a person was an absolute rule in all hunting.

But it was not the anger that confused her. It was the fear. For when Peter had spun around, she happened to see his gaze. The expression in his friendly blue eyes changed in a flash from normal concentration to the sharpness of polished sapphires. She had seen that look many times in hunters in the fraction of a second before they fired.

If the gun had been loaded Tobias could have been dead now.

Embla was not really hungry anymore, but she knew she needed to get something in her stomach before the afternoon post. She made her way toward the grill to get a sausage.

It didn't seem as if the others had noticed what happened.

The manager, Stig Ekström, was standing beside her. Looking for a distraction, she asked, "How's Frippe? Is he very sick?"

"Yes. He's in the hospital with a drip."

"Yikes! What's wrong with him?"

"Ate something. Presumably rat poison. A large quantity. Luckily, what a rat dies from isn't enough to kill a dog."

"But we don't use rat poison. The cabin is insulated," she said.

"There are other buildings that aren't," Ekström muttered. He glared in Sixten's direction.

"Do you know for sure that Sixten uses rat poison?" she asked quietly.

"He did three years ago anyway. He asked to borrow some and I gave him a carton. And he has certainly set out more since then. He hasn't insulated since it's not his cabin."

"Maybe Frippe found rat poison around the Hunting Castle."

"No. We don't use it anymore. I've also insulated the shack and it works fine. That's why I gave Sixten the carton."

Embla was silent a while before she said, "But how could Frippe get into rat poison over here by us? He wasn't around yesterday, was he?"

"Frippe may have found a bigger animal that consumed a sizeable dose and died. Dogs do like carrion."

"True. They can be pretty disgusting."

With a shiver she remembered a death that she and

her colleague had been called to when she was working in a patrol car in central Gothenburg. Her colleague's name was Andreas and back then they worked in the third district. The neighbors had called and complained about a stench from an apartment. It was high summer and they smelled the corpse as soon as they entered the stairwell. When they got up to the apartment they heard muffled growling from the other side of the door. It sounded like a big dog. The locksmith came and picked the lock while she and Andreas cocked their pistols and got into ready position. The locksmith asked to leave before they opened the door. He didn't want to see what was inside, neither corpse nor dog. When Andreas counted to three he pulled open the door. The fetid stench struck them immediately, but no dog came.

They carefully stepped in and closed the door. It was a typical addict's den with mattresses, syringes, empty plastic bags, and all kinds of trash on the floor. The apartment consisted of one room and a kitchen. The door to the bathroom was wide open. Inside the light was on and they saw the dead man lying on the floor. And there was the dog, too: a mixed breed with a lot of Rottweiler. It had survived by drinking water out of the toilet and eating parts of his dead master. The man's entire face was gone.

The dog collapsed beside the corpse, set its head between its paws, and looked at them. As they approached the bathroom it raised its head but didn't growl. Embla met the animal's gaze. Without hesitating she aimed between the eyes and fired.

"What the hell! Why did you shoot the dog?" Andreas screamed.

"Because it asked me to," she answered.

The next day Andreas asked to change assignments; he wanted a new partner in the patrol car.

The scene in the bathroom still haunted her worst nightmares. She had two that constantly recurred. This one wasn't even the worst.

". . . won't be any more hunting for a while."

Suddenly she became aware of Ekström's voice but had no idea what he was talking about. She mumbled in agreement and hurried to swallow the last bite of sausage. Peter and Tobias were looking in her direction and both were trying to get her attention. Right now they were the last two people she wanted to talk to. With long strides she went over to the tree, picked up her rifle and stomped off into the forest.

The rain continued to pour. It felt a little dreary sitting up in the tower, peering out over the rainy, gray forest landscape, but the weather didn't concern her that much. She had hunted in worse conditions. Her anger had started to dissipate, albeit slowly. Damn Tobias! And damn Peter, too! *Peter, yes*. Maybe his behavior could be explained by the fact that he lacked experience, but that was not an acceptable excuse. He had recently taken the hunting test and should have the safety rules fresh in his mind. How could he have been so careless as to break the most important rule?

A barely audible cracking sound made her return to the damp reality in the hunting tower. She stayed stock-still and listened. The sound came from a dense thicket of tall junipers. Carefully, so her clothing wouldn't rustle, she turned herself and the rifle in the direction the sound came from. She supported the rifle against the frame of the tower and twisted the telescopic sight to the largest magnification. At first she didn't see anything, but after a few seconds something moved behind the bushes and a stately bull moose stepped forward. The dewlap was unusually large and its body seemed colossal. In the sight she could see the raindrops on the animal's dense coat.

She had never seen such a fine bull. Her mouth got dry and the familiar feeling of cold spread in her body. *Stay calm, you've done this many times before*, she reminded herself. With her right thumb, she pushed up the safety. *Hold back the shot and wait for the perfect angle*, she thought.

The distance was barely thirty meters. The moose took a few steps forward and stopped. It stood with its rear at an angle to her and sniffed the air suspiciously. In that position it was impossible to shoot. Perhaps it sensed that she was in the vicinity. Slowly the moose turned around. When he was standing completely in profile she fired. The shot went straight through the heart and lungs. The heavy body collapsed on the spot.

Her heart was racing and her whole body felt drained. It took a moment before she could climb down from the tower. She approached her downed prey on shaky legs. Once there she performed something akin to a Native American war dance around the animal's body. She had robbed von Beehn of the sixteen-pointer!

THE HUNTING PARTY had shot seven adult moose and eight calves. Embla's bull was hands down the finest animal. The bull weighed almost exactly 650 kilos and was healthy and in its prime. After inspecting the teeth and horns, Einar and Nisse determined the moose's age to be about twelve years. The horns would get a place of honor over her couch. She had no other hunting trophies on the walls, but this was special.

Seven adult animals and seven calves remained of the quota. They would probably not get that many, but there would be more opportunities during the fall.

Their A license allowed them to hunt for seventy days. There was plenty of time to shoot the remaining moose.

DURING THE EVENING the mood around the dinner table was rather subdued, despite the sixteen-pointer. Tobias whispered to Embla that Peter had apologized to him, but she noted that they still avoided sitting close to each other at the table.

It was horrible that Karin had been bitten by a snake. Everyone had a hard time letting go of the question of how the snake managed to get into the outhouse. They discussed the mystery but did not come to any likely solution. At last it was agreed that it must have slipped in when someone was going in or out of the privy, but Embla didn't think that sounded credible.

They decided that an early bedtime was advisable and the party broke up for the evening. Before Embla turned in, she needed to go out and pee. She crouched behind the junipers. Even though all traces of the dead viper had been swept away, the outhouse did not feel as safe as before.

THE FOLLOWING MORNING was cold and clear. Embla felt the mood rise several degrees. The atmosphere around the breakfast table was markedly lighter.

It was still dark when she took off toward her station with the flashlight in one hand and the rifle hanging from its strap over her shoulder. Even in the beam of the flashlight, the path was hardly visible, but she knew the way well, as she had been sitting in the same tower the last four hunts.

As she approached the tower she heard a pitiful whimper, following by a drawn-out howl that ended in a yelp. She stopped and listened. The sound repeated. A fox. And it was scared and sad. Carefully she moved forward with her flashlight. The whine stopped abruptly when the animal perceived her presence, but she could still hear it struggling. Then she saw the awful scene. The fox's terrified eyes stared right into the light. Around its mouth, foam edged with blood. One hind leg was stuck in a big foot-hold trap, and it looked as if the leg was almost completely severed. Blood surrounded the trap; the fox had tried to bite off its leg to get loose.

She had never seen a foot-hold trap in the area before. For a long time it had been illegal to hunt with them.

With trembling fingers she grabbed her two-way radio. "Embla here. Below my tower there's a fox stuck in a big foot-hold trap. It's severely injured. I'm going to kill it. Over and out."

There were a few moments of silence.

"A foot-hold trap? Are you sure?" she heard Sixten say.

"Absolutely."

"Okay, then. Shoot. But Nisse and I are coming over to you to see what the hell is going on. The rest of you wait till I return. Over and out!"

After fifteen minutes the two men were there. In silence they stood and looked at the dead fox. Seppo was tied to a tree and made it clear that she would also really like to take a closer look.

"My God! Not even my old man used foot-hold traps. They're terrible!" Sixten exclaimed.

"I agree. This is an old trap. Rather large, but certainly intended for foxes or beavers. But how did the trap end up here?" said Nisse.

They looked at each other in the faint light of dawn. It would be a beautiful morning, but neither of them were able to appreciate it at the moment.

"It wasn't here yesterday. I would have seen it because it's lying right on the path," said Embla.

Nisse's knee creaked as he crouched and examined the trap and the ground around it. He looked very serious when he stood up again.

"It was well-hidden under moss and leaves."

"Who does something so fucking dangerous?" Sixten looked around combatively, as if he hoped to catch sight of the guilty party somewhere among the spruce trees.

"Someone who wants to sabotage or injure. And I

wonder . . . Embla, you're the only one who uses this path," said Nisse.

She swallowed a few times before she could answer. "I'll take a few pictures with my phone. This is a hunting violation," she said, trying to sound unperturbed.

"Yes, and it could just as well have been you who stepped right on the trap. Even if your leg hadn't been severed, you still would have been injured."

"Do you think I should report it?" she asked.

"Absolutely," Nisse said grimly.

SIXTEN SUMMONED THE hunters to the grilling area. He recounted what had happened and showed them the foot-hold trap. It was a rather clumsy trap made of rusty iron and a sturdy chain. At the end of it was an iron rod that anchors the trap to the ground so the prey can't run away with the jaws of the trap on its foot. The mechanism was in good shape: it was well-lubricated and closed with a powerful snap when Sixten pressed on the pan with a thick branch. Wood chips flew as it snapped shut.

Most of the hunters had never seen a foot-hold trap, much less owned one. None of them had noticed anything suspicious either the night before or that morning.

"We won't get anywhere with this right now. Let's go back to our stations. But keep an eye out for any more traps, everyone. This one is going to be investigated," Sixten said.

IT TURNED OUT to be a fine day for hunting, even if they only shot one calf. They gathered at the Hunting Castle where Sixten thanked the two parties for a successful hunt.

Tobias and Einar crammed into Peter's car so that the ones who were staying another day could borrow their pickup. They needed it to transport the animals that were shot to the shed for butchering. Peter's new car didn't have a towing hook, but he promised to remedy that for the following year.

The members of von Beehn's hunting party were already done packing. Stig Ekström would drive them in the Hummer to Dalsnäs where their cars were. On Thursday he would have the day off and wouldn't return in the Hummer until Friday morning. The King Cab would stay behind at von Beehn's cabin in case Anders and Jan-Eric needed a vehicle.

On Wednesday evening only Embla, Nisse, and Sixten were sitting in the main room having dinner together. Sixten brought out a couple of strong beers that he maintained he had reserved for that night. The other two were a bit surprised; he was not one who was in the habit of sharing, especially where alcoholic beverages were concerned. Embla declined the beer but Nisse took one. He had made a sausage casserole from all the different things that were left over. A can of crushed tomatoes, ketchup, onion, and a dollop of cream did the trick. Along with rice it turned out to be surprisingly good. Sixten took generous helpings, both of the sausage casserole and of the beer. When he was on his third can he looked at Embla with half-closed eyes. With his coarse fist he rubbed his face several times so the beard stubble scraped before he dove in.

"You should watch out for that Peter. There's something shady about him."

"What do you mean, 'shady'?" She tried to look innocent but could feel that her cheeks were getting hot.

"Everyone wonders why he came back. But I know. He's got some mischief in mind." As if to confirm his own statement he nodded several times. Then, with an audible slurp, he finished the last drops in the can.

"What kind of mischief? Now you have to explain," said Nisse.

She was grateful that he was asking questions too, it would make the conversation feel more relaxed than an interrogation. Because that was exactly what she felt she wanted to hold with Sixten: an interrogation. He and Peter had circled each other like two barracudas the past few days. It was time to find out the reason.

Instead of answering he stood up and went for two more cans of beer. At first Nisse looked hesitant, but after quickly sneaking a glance in Embla's direction he knew it was crucial to get Sixten to tell what was behind the animosity between the two men. And for once it seemed as if he really wanted to talk, perhaps even felt a need to.

After several deep gulps Sixten wiped off the foam from the beard stubble with the back of his fist. "Mischief? Yeah, let me tell you! The bastard has cameras set up everywhere. No one can approach Hansgården without being filmed. He says that it's because of all the computers he has in the house. He's afraid of thieves. But I think he has something else going on. Child pornography or something!"

"Hansgården is rather isolated. No one would see if there was a burglary—" Nisse objected, but Sixten interrupted him.

"He has alarms, too. Not just in the house but in the surrounding buildings and the stable."

No one else in the area had burglar alarms, not even in their houses. There was no point: before the closest security company would arrive, the house would be emptied. You have to rely on neighborly cooperation, which wasn't always so simple. Often the distance between farms was so great that they were not within sight of each other.

"How do you know all this?" Nisse asked.

Sixten struck his knuckles against his chest and belched audibly before he replied. "Alarm-Gösta in Bengtsfors who installed everything told me."

Embla could not keep from smiling. In the countryside there were no secrets. She jumped in again. "But Peter works a lot from home. The computers and all the other equipment must be expensive."

In response Sixten glared at her but did not reply. It was obvious that he didn't buy that argument. "Explain that business with the room then!" A crafty smile slipped across his thin lips and he screwed up one eye.

"The room?" Embla and Nisse said in unison.

Sixten grinned contentedly at the effect and lowered his voice. "The carpenters who did the renovation weren't allowed to go into one of the rooms. Now that's shady!"

Embla exchanged a quick glance with her uncle but didn't say anything. After a moment's silence Nisse asked, "How do you know they weren't allowed to?"

"Mattsson's Construction had the contract. Patrik Mattsson said that it was so damn strange. He spent money on everything else in the house. Only the best and most expensive. But one room was always locked. No one could go in there."

Embla tried to sound disinterested as she asked, "Where in the house is that locked room? The basement, or what?"

Sixten's bushy eyebrows were knit together and his forehead had deep folds; he was truly trying to think. "Don't know. I didn't ask," he said at last.

THURSDAY DAWNED AS clear as the day before. After consultation the five remaining hunters decided to devote the day to deer hunting. But hard rain interrupted the hunt at three o'clock, and they drove the day's kill down to the shed to prepare the deer carcasses. Afterward they drove back to unhook the cart and park it by the cabins. Anders von Beehn and Jan-Eric Cahneborg took off toward the Hunting Castle, while the three others started getting ready for the trip home.

When everything was packed they got in the car and started driving back down toward the shed. Deep ruts in the forest road from the last few days of driving slowed their progress. After a few heavy autumn rains the road would become almost unpassable. That was the main reason the new shed had been placed down by the gravel road, whereas the old shed had been much closer to the hunting cabins. The transports to the new shed may take longer, but at least they weren't as difficult to navigate when the rains set in.

Embla thought it was fun to drive the big pickup. Compared to her old Volvo there was a completely different kind of comfort. The truck could make its way anywhere. Neither she nor Nisse talked; they didn't want to disturb Sixten, who was in the backseat, sound asleep.

He had turned seventy in January. He didn't have a party because his only living relative was an older sister in a home for the elderly Stockholm. Neither of them had any children, so there was no one to inherit his farm.

Embla pulled into the yard in front of Karin and Björn's house, and both of them came out on the stoop. Her cousin looked tired and Embla asked how she was feeling.

"Not too bad. Better. But it still feels stiff and tender."

Karin showed them her hand. The two points were still visible, but the swelling had started to go down. When she heard about the foot-hold trap that had been hidden on the path she turned pale. "Has anyone figured out how the snake got into the outhouse?" she asked after a while.

"No. It's strange. It's insulated everywhere."

Something glistened in Karin's gaze and she leaned forward to whisper to Embla.

"Someone put it there. It fits in with the foot-hold trap. There's a lunatic running around up there!"

Embla frowned. "Why would someone—?"

"No idea."

A foolish joke, perhaps? No, that didn't make sense. All the men in the hunting party were relatives and friends. The thought that someone in von Beehn's group would be amused by that kind of practical joke was not likely either. No one would do something that stupid and dangerous.

When everything had been unloaded from the truck, Embla went up to the shower room on the top floor and undressed. She let the clothes fall in a heap on the floor and then stepped into the shower. As she shampooed her hair the smell of sweat, earth, and smoke was released. The smell of hunting. It made her long for the forest. In a day and a half they would be back in the cabin. She was already looking forward to it.

Her clean clothes were on the bed. It was a nice feeling to put them on. She took the pile of dirty laundry down to the laundry room and stuffed everything into the washing machine. It would have to go nonstop all evening.

Out in the kitchen Nisse was preparing dinner. Without turning around he said, "Because this is Thursday you'll get pea soup and pancakes with my homemade raspberry jam."

"Good! I can mind the soup."

On the counter beside the stove she saw two plastic bags of prepared pea soup. She could certainly manage to cut open the plastic, squeeze the soup out into a saucepan, add a little water, and heat it. And as the dot over the *i* she would add lots of home-grown thyme from a pot on the windowsill.

The kitchen had been renovated in the late 1970s. It was all in pine, with rustic cupboard doors and drawers. They had replaced the stove, dishwasher, and refrigerator a year or so ago. Embla had tried to convince him to put in a completely new kitchen, but Nisse didn't want to. He was comfortable in his pine kitchen. The only thing he agreed to do something about was the floor, which he had sanded and stained.

They made conversation about everything imaginable while they cooked. At last they inevitably came to what they were both wondering about. It was Nisse who brought it up.

"What do you think Peter Hansson is up to?"

"He works in IT. The insurance company probably requires alarms . . ."

"Don't play dumb! The secret room," he said with a snort.

He knew her much too well. That damn room had been swirling around in her head ever since Sixten had told about it. Why does someone have a locked room that no one can go into? Obviously because you don't want anyone to see what you have going on. It could be as simple as he handled confidential and sensitive information on behalf of his clients and needed to protect it. But in purely practical terms, wouldn't that room too have been in need of renovation before it was put into use? Why couldn't the tradesmen go into it? Perhaps he had constructed a gigantic train set over the whole floor where he ran Märklin trains and didn't want that to be gossiped about in the village, but he didn't really seem to be the type. But what type was he?

"Do you think I should take a closer look at Peter and that room?"

Nisse did not reply immediately. He was completely focused on turning a golden brown pancake. Embla watched as he tossed it with an elegant flip of the wrist up in the air and caught it in the frying pan again. When the pancake had landed safely and started sizzling in the butter he turned around and looked at her thoughtfully. "You haven't taken a shine to him, have you?"

She felt a slight double-stroke in the heart region . . . had she? Peter was good-looking and attractive, while at the same time a bit inaccessible and contradictory. "I admit that I may feel a bit interested. He's good-looking and . . . but there's something else. He's . . . interesting."

"Hmm. Interesting. Do you mean the cop in you is curious, perhaps?" Nisse turned around again and raised the finished pancake with the spatula, placing it on top of the stack. With his finger he carefully scraped the batter together in the bowl to make one last pancake.

"Well, yes, people with secrets are always interesting, don't you think?" she said.

She could not stop brooding about what Peter was doing in the secret room. If there even *was* such a room, maybe it was just loose talk. She was so submerged in her thoughts that she forgot to stir the soup. At the last moment Nisse noticed it and pulled the saucepan off the burner.

"Oh! Is it still edible?"

"Of course. We don't need to eat what's on the bottom."

AFTER DINNER THEY sat bloated and content in front of the TV. It was seven-thirty, time for the news. Normally Embla tried to keep up with current events, but her thoughts were much too distracted by a locked secret room. Finally she turned toward Nisse.

"Will you help out if I check out Peter and his mysterious room later tonight?"

"Try to stop me," he said with a smile.

Hansgården was almost five kilometers from Nisse's farm and Embla's plan was based on the fact that it was that far away. To help her she had Nisse, Seppo, and her old Volvo. No preparations were needed other than removing the gas can that was always kept filled in the luggage compartment of the Veteran.

As the time approached eight they were ready to get going. She sprayed on a little perfume and brushed some layers of mascara on her eyelashes. For protection from the cold she put on a knit cardigan over a black T-shirt with a deep neckline that she had changed into.

By the time she walked to the car, it was pitch-black outside and rain was hanging in the air. She tossed her thick jacket, mittens, and cap into the backseat. Under the passenger seat she hid a pair of binoculars. There they would be easily accessible but not visible if someone were to look into the car. She put her cell phone in the pocket of her jacket. Carefully she went through the plan with Nisse. He was attentive and understood exactly.

If she hadn't seen the expression in Peter's eyes when he aimed the rifle at Tobias she probably wouldn't have agreed to the plan. The experience had been upsetting and she never wanted to be part of anything like it again.

And if she was now more than just interested in him, it was important to find out what he was hiding. Computers that spit out the most disgusting kinds of pornography, orchid cultivation, marijuana plants, model train tracks . . . ? She had to find out.

Half a kilometer from Hansgården, Embla slowed down and parked the car far out on the edge of the road. When she peered through the binoculars she saw that there were lights on behind the lowered blinds in one of the windows on the top floor. Otherwise the house was dark. The area around the three buildings on the farm was brightly lit up by several floodlights. It would be impossible to sneak up toward any of the buildings under the cover of darkness.

After taking a deep breath she got out of the car and took out two warning triangles from the luggage compartment. One she placed a little ways in front of the car, the other a little behind.

With purposeful steps she walked toward Hansgården. She didn't detect any movement behind the blinds on the top floor. Right before she stepped into the light that fell across the yard, she took out her phone and called Nisse. As agreed he did not answer. With an oath she put the phone away again. It was important to look believable in case Peter was watching her from behind one of the dark windows. As she came closer her pulse increased. She was nervous. It didn't get better when she suddenly felt something moving by her lower leg. With a suppressed cry she started. Relieved, she saw that it was a red-striped cat that had brushed against her. It slipped past her and disappeared behind the corner of the house.

The freshly painted blue front door was equipped with

a digital lock and a sturdy cast-iron door knocker. Firmly she knocked the clapper three times against the plate. Behind the door everything was quiet. When she had waited quite some time she rapped on the door again: *ta-ta-ta-ta-ta-ta* echoed from inside the house. After another minute or so she took her phone out of her jacket pocket. In the corner of her eye she noticed a camera hanging over the door, but she pretended she hadn't seen it. Instead she called Nisse's cell phone again. After a few ringtones he answered.

"This is Nisse."

"Hi. It's me. I've run out of gas and of course I forgot the gas can. It's still in the garage. Now I'm standing outside the door to Hansgården. It doesn't look like Peter is at home. And I haven't seen the dog."

She fell silent and listened to what Nisse said.

"The soonest in half an hour . . . an hour, okay. So they've seen Seppo? That's great! Then maybe you'll get ahold of him . . . Okay, I'll wait half an hour at most by the car. If it takes longer I'll walk over to Karin and Björn's, so you can go there with the can and pick me up . . . Yes, that's fine."

She clicked off the call and raised her hand to the cast-iron ring for a third and final time. At the same moment the door soundlessly swung open on well-oiled hinges, leaving her standing there with a raised fist. Peter stood in the doorway smiling at her. His hair was wet and he was barefoot and dressed in jeans and a red T-shirt.

"Hello there! What are you doing here?"

He sounded sincerely happy.

"I'm out looking for Seppo. He ran off. And I drove in this direction . . . and now I've run out of gas."

"I see. And where's the car?"

"A short distance away. Half a kilometer maybe. The fuel gauge is broken and I forgot the extra can. It's usually in the back of the car but it got a little stressful and . . ." With an apologetic smile and a shrug, she did not complete the sentence.

"I understand. Come in. I hope you'll have a cup of tea because I intended to have one myself."

"That sounds great. Thanks."

She stepped across the threshold and he closed the door behind her.

"Unfortunately I only have alkylate gasoline in the outbuilding. For the lawnmower. Environmentally sound," he said.

"It's probably not worth putting it in the Veteran then. He'd just choke."

"The Veteran?"

"The car. It's twenty-four years old."

"Impressive!"

"Yes. Although it does have a few issues—the fuel gauge, for one."

The hall was roomy without any furnishings other than a closet that peeked out behind sliding doors of mirrored glass. The light-gray granite floor tiles were tinged with warm pink. When she had taken off her shoes, she could feel the heat from the coils under the stone. A few spotlights in the hall were on, but the rest of the house was still submerged in darkness. He took her jacket and hung it up on the hat rack behind the sliding door.

"Excuse me for not answering right away. I was taking a shower."

That was somewhat superfluous information considering his bare feet and damp hair, thought Embla.

"I didn't think you were home. The house was completely dark. Or well, there was a light in a window on the top floor . . ."

"The office. I was working. Then I forget to turn on the rest of the lights. But now there will be light!" From the pocket of his jeans he took out an iPhone and poked at it a few times with his index finger. Spotlights came on all over the house, and it immediately felt much cozier.

"You have a smart house," she observed.

"Of course. I was actually involved in developing the technology. Modern homes are full of electronics and small computers. And because it's my job . . . voilà." He threw out his hands, looking like a magician who was expecting applause after a skillfully performed trick.

"So can you, like, turn on the tea kettle with your phone?"

"Yes, actually. Although it's important to remember to always keep the kettle filled. Same with the coffeemaker." He quickly tapped on his iPhone a few more times.

"So with your phone you can control the stove, the refrigerator, the furnace . . ."

"Yes, you name it. I can be anywhere in the world and still have complete control of my house. And I can let people in, like repairmen, when I'm not home."

Although you should never do that, the detective in her thought, but she didn't say it out loud. Instead she asked, "All that's required is that the electronics are connected to some type of computer, right?"

"A modern cell phone is enough. It's actually a small

computer. Then you just need smart plugs in the outlets for the electrical devices you want to turn on and off."

He smiled and made an inviting gesture with his hand that she should step into the kitchen. Sure enough, an electric tea kettle was bubbling away on the stone counter. He took out a teapot from a cupboard and placed it beside the kettle. He grabbed a metal filter and measured out tea from a lovely tin that looked old.

"I only have Earl Grey," he said.

"That's fine."

"So you don't just drink herbal tea?"

"No. Although I don't like green tea."

While they talked she took the opportunity to discreetly look around the kitchen. The lower cabinets had smooth, glossy white doors, while the upper ones were equipped with glass doors. Spotlights inside the cabinets made the glass and porcelain glisten. The appliances were stainless steel. Everything was new and of modern design. The floor was the same kind of granite tile as in the hall; it seemed as if the stone floor covered the entire downstairs. *Nice, he has good taste*, she thought. She herself never would have come up with such well-thought-out décor. She didn't have time, interest, or money for that matter.

"Unfortunately I only have some frozen store-bought rolls to offer. Or would you like a cheese sandwich?"

"No, thanks. We had a late dinner."

"Dinner . . . that reminds me. I forgot about that. Then it will have to be a sandwich for me." He pointed toward a wide doorway and said, "Please, go and have a seat, and I'll join you shortly."

Probably not enough time to have a look around, Embla

thought, and she followed his instructions. On her way toward the big room she passed the glassed-in veranda. It was a decent size; presumably it had been expanded during the renovation. The dining room was there, with a substantial table of oiled oak and six matching leather-clad chairs. Above the table a small chandelier sparkled with holders for candles.

The L-shaped living room was impressive; she had a strong feeling that this room, too, had been expanded. A large soapstone stove towered in the inside corner of the L. In front of it were two dark-gray leather swivel armchairs and a small, round smoke-colored coffee table. At the far end of the room she saw an elegant sofa, upholstered in light-gray linen fabric, and a second coffee table, this time oval, with a wrought-iron frame and a sturdy top of dark-gray marble. Over the table a large, wrought-iron chandelier was hanging with glass candle holders. Almost the entire wall above the sofa was covered by a gigantic oil painting in various shades of blue and green with patches of white. The painting depicted an agitated sea where the storm whipped up foam like smoke from the crests of the waves. The sea felt threatening and mighty and had a powerful effect on Embla. It was the only painting she had seen so far in the house.

She sat down in one of the armchairs in front of the stove. Through the glass in the door, she could see a neatly stacked wood pile, and a box of long matches were above the stove.

"Should I light the fire?" she called so that he would hear her out in the kitchen.

"Absolutely."

She bounced in the chair when she heard his voice right behind her; she hadn't heard him come in.

Carefully he set down two red-glazed mugs on the glass table. "Milk? Sugar?"

"Neither, thanks."

When he turned and went back to the kitchen she stood up and took the matchbox from the shelf. She opened the door and struck a match. Before she lit the fire, she hesitated. Under the wood were large wads of paper. She took a quick look at them: financial pages from a newspaper. Nothing interesting. She lit the papers and returned to her seat.

This time she was more on her guard and heard his steps approach. Quickly she arranged her face into a friendly smile before she turned around.

"What a great stove!"

"Yes. Efficient. Finnish. The soapstone retains the heat for a very long time. It gets so warm you can cook food on it. Practical in case of a power outage."

"You've thought of everything."

He gave her a contented look and smiled but did not reply. He set down a small pitcher of milk and a tray with a large open-faced cheese sandwich on the glass table. On top of the cheese were two rings of red pepper, two tomato wedges, and some cucumber slices. To top it off he had set a sprig of parsley. *This guy is too heavily trained!* was the thought that passed through her mind. *And he's a mind reader too!* She didn't share either thought.

"You've done such a nice job with the house." She said, mostly to change the subject, but she meant it.

"Yes, it turned out well if I do say so myself." Greedily he sank his teeth into the sandwich.

"When you have a space like this, I can see why you prefer to work from home," she continued.

"That was the idea with this renovation: create an environment that was just mine."

"It's great. Really great!"

"Thanks."

They sat quietly for a while and watched the fire crackle and jump behind the glass door.

Once Peter had finished his sandwich, he leaned back in the chair and inspected her. "Does Seppo run away often?"

It was a question she was prepared for. "According to Nisse it's happened a time or two before. For the same reason. Ladies. He'll be three years old soon. Now he knows what's going on when his lady friends start smelling irresistible."

"Personally I was probably a few years older . . ."

Their eyes met and she felt that she was starting to blush. She seldom did that, and she felt a little confused. At the same moment her phone rang, and was relieved to have somewhere else to direct her attention.

"Sorry, it's Nisse. One moment," she said to Peter as she slid the button on her phone to accept the call. "Hi, Nisse . . . That's great! Then you just have to retrieve him . . . Okay!"

With a satisfied expression she clicked off the phone. Damn. How quickly the time had passed. She hadn't even been in the vicinity of the top floor or anything resembling a locked room.

"Nisse has a lead on Seppo. Karin called and said he's in their neighbor's garden and refuses to move. They have a fat, old female dachshund who is apparently in heat."

There was no risk that Peter would see through the lie because there really was an old dachshund at Karin and Björn's neighbor's house. The elderly couple who owned the dachshund usually let her out in the yard to do her business. What the dog got up to then, no one could say for certain. A meeting with a considerably younger admirer was completely possible.

"Ah, well, you know what they say. Love is blind," said Peter.

"True. But Nisse said he's coming with the gas can in around twenty minutes."

"Then you have time for another cup."

"No, thanks. But I do need to use the restroom."

"Sure. Come, let me show you."

He got up and went ahead of her toward the hall. She had already seen the bathroom door when she came in, but she also remembered a door somewhat farther away. To catch up with Peter she hurried her pace and started talking.

"Will you be able to come up to hunt on Saturday?"

"I will. I'm getting home late tomorrow night, but that's no problem . . . No, not that one!"

The last comment had a sharp edge to it. With a few quick steps she had crossed the hall and gone up to the door she had seen earlier. Quickly she pulled down the handle, simply to confirm that it was locked. Beside the doorframe was yet another digital lock. She giggled and said with surprise, "Oh! Have you locked the bathroom door?"

"No. That's the door to the bathroom over there."

With a blank expression he pointed toward the door in the hall.

With some embarrassed apologies she went into the bathroom. To be on the safe side she pulled down her jeans and sat down on the seat. She had to play her role well, down to the slightest detail. With some effort she managed to squeeze out a squirt.

When she came out again she saw he had put on shoes and a sweater.

"I'll go with you. You don't have a flashlight," he said.

His voice sounded normal again.

She put on her jacket and they went out on the front steps. Peter pressed lightly on his phone display and she could hear the door locking behind them. In silence they started walking toward her car.

When she took hold of the handle to the locked door the trust between them had cracked. It was clumsy, she knew, but at the same time it had been important to find out whether the rumor about the locked room was true. And it was. And it was worse than that: the door to the whole top floor was locked.

"Why do you lock the door to the top floor?" she asked.

Without sounding the least bit hesitant, he answered, "The insurance company requires locks everywhere. As I've told you, I work on security issues for various companies, and there's a major risk of industrial espionage. Millions, sometimes billions is at stake. The computers and other equipment that I have at home also cost a lot of money."

"I see." She tried to sound as if she weren't particularly interested, but the doubt remained.

When they came up to the car her uncle was already there, filling the Veteran's tank from a big metal can.

He said hello to them and blinked in the sharp light from the flashlight. Peter lowered the beam of light toward the ground and returned the greeting. Embla went up to Nisse's Mazda and looked into the backseat. With a happy bark Seppo jumped up and pressed her nose against the window. To his surprise she started scolding him.

"Naughty pup! Running off in the dark to go courting! That lady is much too old for you!"

Seppo lowered his tail and looked unhappy—not because he understood what she was saying, but because he could tell from her tone that she wasn't pleased.

"Now you have enough gas to take you a few kilometers. Don't forget to fill her up," said Nisse.

"Thanks so much, you're an angel!"

He went back to his own car and his bewildered dog. With a roaring start he drove toward a turnout a dozen or so meters away and made a U turn.

When the taillights of the Mazda had disappeared down the road, she turned toward Peter. He had turned off the flashlight. Now she could only see his silhouette a little ways from her.

"Thanks for the tea."

"Yes, that was very nice. See you Saturday."

Before she could say anything else, he had turned on his heels and started walking back toward the house. With a sigh she picked up the two warning triangles. Then one last glance toward the house made her stop. The indirect light from all the spotlights illuminated the whole bottom floor with a warm glow. It really was an extremely fine house he had built for himself.

"WHAT DO YOU think? What kind of shady business is he involved in?" Nisse was looking at her urgently over the edge of his teacup.

"No idea. He says he has to protect his computers and client information . . . and that sounds credible. But . . ." She fell silent and sipped her hot tea. "I don't know . . . maybe it's him. One moment he's as sweet and easygoing as anything. The next moment it's like he closes himself off and turns . . . cold."

Nisse scrutinized her through narrowed eyes. He knew her well, and it was not just in appearance that they resembled each other. "You would like him to be sweet through and through and . . . what did you say . . . easy-going. But there are actually very few people who are. All the time, I mean."

"I know. But there's something else."

He gave her a thoughtful look. "He has a responsible, stressful job. And perhaps he has a dark side. It runs in his family," he said.

Embla's feet were starting to get numb because Seppo's head was lying on them. He'd been lying that way ever since they got home. According to Nisse it was because the dog was eager for them to be friends again after the scolding in the car. It was impossible to explain to a dog that it had all been just theater. Dogs don't lie and play act; they always show their true feelings. Truthfully, she was ashamed of the trickery she and Nisse had staged. Peter had the right to privacy. She herself was not someone who ran around shouting out her own secrets.

Someone who had to pay the price for that was Lollo.

AT LONG LAST there was peace and quiet in the house. Jan-Eric had fallen asleep after dinner, but he would soon wake up again and insist on some sandwiches, accompanied by aquavit and beer. And obviously they would continue to discuss the questions that they had dwelled on over the past twenty-four hours: Who was M? It couldn't be . . . No. Absolutely not. So who was it? And what were the sender's intentions? Probably blackmail, they were in agreement on that. But why right now? And why had they received the key ring and the scarf? Or the bandanna, as Jan-Eric persisted in calling it. Sure, in their youth they had had a certain connection to the things they received in the envelopes, but that was a very long time ago. So why . . . why . . . why?

The questions played through Anders von Beehn's mind as he plopped down on the bed. It was impossible to rest. His gaze fell on the book on the nightstand. It was worth a try. He took his reading glasses out of their case, set them far down on his nose, and puffed up the pillows against the head of the bed. A dose of business law would surely calm his overheated brain.

But he had a hard time concentrating on the text. Images of the BMW key ring and the slip of paper that said "I remember. M" kept gliding across the pages of the book.

Jan-Eric started moving around in his room. Anders heard him swear audibly as he searched for something in the mess. Anders put down his reading and pressed on his cell phone. The screen lit up and showed that it was 11:21. Heavy steps approached his door and stopped.

"I'm going out to pee," Jan-Eric announced.

"Do that. I'm just going to finish reading. Then I'll go down and take out the sandwiches."

"Marvelous!"

Anders heard his friend's steps go away in the direction of the stairs.

There was only half a page left in the chapter, it would be just right to stop there. With all the concentration he could muster he started reading again.

After a minute or so he heard a sound. It came from outside and sounded like a cry. A human one. Quickly he set the book down on the nightstand and took off his glasses. With the phone in his hand he went up to the window.

At first he didn't see anything, just total darkness. His gaze was attracted to the only source of light out there, the lantern by the precipice overlooking the lake.

At the outer edge of the circle of light, turned away from him, stood M.

Impossible! He dropped the phone on the dresser by the window. Without thinking he went over to the little closet where he kept his Carl Gustaf, took out the gun, and loaded it robotically.

It was only as he went down the stairs that he asked

himself why he had taken the rifle. If the person he had seen was still out there, the gun would not be of any help. The only thing that could possibly protect him was a skillful medium.

After a night's restless sleep, Embla got up right before seven and pulled on her running clothes, cap, and mittens. It was a cold, clear morning, with the thermometer showing two degrees below freezing. The rain that had fallen the night before had frozen, so she had to watch out for ice on the puddles.

She put in the earbuds from her iPod and started jogging lightly to warm up. Her favorite song to run to was The Streets' "Fit But You Know It." Kolbjörn had tipped her off about the band almost ten years ago, and since then she preferred to run to their music. In recent years their rap and hip-hop had a bit of a harder edge, and the music gave her energy.

When she realized that she was on her way toward Hansgården, she was a little embarrassed at first. It was obvious that she was drawn toward the farm. Or perhaps its owner. But she continued in that direction.

She decided to turn when Hansgården started to be visible. She definitely did not want Peter to see her. And the five kilometers there and back was a more than adequate distance to run. Before she turned back she stopped to catch her breath for a few seconds. As she was about to start running again she glanced toward the farm. A yellow sports car turned out from the farmyard and came right toward her at high speed. It was extremely souped-up and seemed like it was lapping up the road. It must be Peter's other car. Naturally he didn't drive the Range Rover when he was going to meet clients in Gothenburg. A Ferrari made a completely different impression.

As he approached he slowed down and stopped completely when he was even with her. The window glided down.

"Hi. Did you run out of gas again?"

"No. Just running . . ."

She was intensely aware of the sweat sticking under the running clothes and cap. Peter looked like an advertisement for some exclusive menswear store. There was also a light whiff of a pleasing masculine aroma coming through the open window.

"Listen, we have something to clear up. Jump in," he said. He leaned across the passenger seat and opened the door.

"But I . . ."

"Jump in."

Decisively she rounded the car and crouched down to slide in. To hide her embarrassment she laughed. "Good thing I'm flexible."

He simply hummed. Quickly he backed up toward the turnout and made a U turn as Nisse had done the night before, although in the opposite direction. At high speed he drove back toward Hansgården. With squealing tires he stopped the car abruptly at the front steps. Without a word he got out of the car and went up the steps. The red cat slipped after him and started strutting around his legs. Impatiently he chased it away while he entered the code and opened the door. Only then did he turn around to look at her. She had just managed to get out of the car but remained standing by it and gave him a puzzled look.

"Come on," he said, nodding toward the house.

Hesitantly she started walking up the steps. When she came into the hall he had already opened the door that she had tugged on the night before. With an exaggerated gesture he waved toward the steps behind it.

"Please step in."

It was impossible to miss the sarcasm.

"Such an honor," she said in the same tone of voice.

She felt a light burning pain in her stomach but wasn't sure if it was because she hadn't had any breakfast or if it could be traced to something else. Courteously he let her go up the steps first. She was intensely aware of the odor of sweat she left behind her.

When they came up to a bright hallway, she turned toward him and said, "Why did you take me here?"

"Because this is where you wanted to go yesterday. There's not a chance that you mistook the bathroom door for this one. And the questions you asked. You wanted to see what was up here and now you'll get to." He went up to a door that was equipped with a digital lock. The lock buzzed before he opened it.

"My office."

When she peeked into the room she got a light nudge on the back.

"Step in."

"Okay, okay. But what do you really want?" She twirled around and glared furiously at him.

The look he gave her was contemptuous, as was the

tone in his voice when he answered. "I want you to see what's in here so the bullshit stops."

It felt like a slap. But he was right. Gossip and rumors were the reason for her performance the night before.

Instead of saying anything she looked around the large room. It was painted completely white, even the floorboards. The beams in the ceiling were exposed to make it feel more spacious. In the middle of the room there were two desks facing each other with various computers, monitors, printers, and even some speakers. One wall was taken up by an enormous screen. A gigantic speaker system covered the floor below it. Besides the lights over the desks and two black leather office chairs, the room was otherwise completely empty. Not even a Post-it note was visible by the computers or on the walls.

"You don't have any bookcases," she noted.

"No, why should I? I download what I want to read on my iPad or phone. There isn't a paper book in the whole house."

"So this is where you sit and work all day long."

"Exactly. When I'm not in Gothenburg or meeting clients abroad somewhere."

There was nothing that seemed shady. On the contrary the room looked quite sterile. But who knew what was on those computers.

"Of course I can't show you what I have on the computers. Everything is confidential."

Once again she got the feeling that he could read her thoughts.

"I knocked out a wall between two bedrooms to make the room large enough. Otherwise there's just my bedroom, a small guest room, and a bathroom up here."

"Yes, you have plenty of space."

He nodded and inquisitively raised his eyebrows. "Are you satisfied with what you've seen in here?" he said.

"Yes. Thanks."

The whole situation felt unpleasant and strange, but she kept a straight face. He walked across the polished floor of the hall and opened another door, which also was equipped with a digital lock.

"The bedroom," he said, again making an exaggerated gesture toward the room.

Why did he need a lock on the bedroom door? Hesitantly she stepped across the threshold. The morning light shone in through the balcony windows and flooded across a wide bed. It was neatly made with a light-gray quilt and some dark violet silk pillows that matched a thick, fluffy bedside rug. It was the first rug she had seen in the house. On the high headboard was a two-armed bed lamp. One wall was covered by black, opaque glass sliding doors that, presumably, concealed closets.

"Such a nice room!"

"Yes."

She went up to the balcony doors and looked out the windows. The autumn colors dominated the peaceful landscape, which was lit up by the crooked rays of the morning sun. It looked like it was going to be a really fine day.

The aroma of Peter's aftershave got stronger and his voice was suddenly right behind her.

"And as you surely know I also have alarms on the barn and the outbuilding. Do you want to inspect them, too?"

His tone dripped with sarcasm. She felt anger rising inside her. She turned around and gave him a hard look.

"What makes you think you're so damn interesting that everyone is talking about you? Sure, I took the opportunity to look around the house last night. I'm a cop. It's a hard habit to shake. But it was for my own curiosity. I wasn't snooping on behalf of the whole village. Sorry if my presence upset you, but I can promise that it won't be repeated!" Angrily she marched out of the room.

"Then I assume you don't care to inspect the guest room?" she heard him say behind her back.

She could still hear the sarcasm in his voice. Anger flared up as she ran down the steep stairs. Her face was flushed and she needed to get out in the fresh air. With a jerk she got the front door open and stepped out. For a moment she stopped and took a few deep breaths, which made her heart rate decrease and her thoughts clear somewhat. Forcing herself to be calm, she started jogging back the way she had come.

The anger started to give way to the insight that she hadn't handled the situation very professionally. As usual, her anxiety had taken over when she started to feel foolish. She should have kept a cool head. And yesterday's stunt when she had "ran out of gas" was not exactly a high point where her acting talents were concerned. The only important result was that she had gotten to see some of Peter's less appealing traits. As Nisse had pointed out, we all have our dark sides. Peter's was evidently that he lacked the ability to let people get close to him. He distrusted them—that was apparent, and he seemed almost a little paranoid. And here she had imagined the two of them were trying to get to know each other, that they both wanted . . . What *had* she imagined actually?

The guy must be completely out of his mind, isolating himself on a farm in the middle of nowhere and pumping a fortune into the renovation of the buildings, cars that cost several years' income for a normal farmer here in the area, and locked rooms and . . . well, what? People didn't know that much more about him. Sure, he looks good.

Damn!

The sound of the spinning engine of the Ferrari cut into her thoughts as it approached from behind. She continued running at the same pace. The sports car passed without slowing down. The gravel sprayed around the tires, and she was forced to stop. It took a while before the coughing subsided and her eyes stopped tearing up.

EMBLA WENT FOR a hard, hour-long bout with Nisse's punching bag and speed ball out in the barn. As she stood in the shower her thoughts started to clear. She had to admit to herself that she was more than just interested, as she had said to Nisse. She was starting to fall for the mysterious hottie. It felt as if the air between them was vibrating with feelings, both positive and negative. Which was incredibly silly, she knew, since they hardly knew each other. And in the beginning he had given signals that he was interested, too, before suddenly changing course and turning unpleasant. It was obvious he didn't want any close contact with other people. So why had he given her hints, such as inviting her to the farm? Had she misinterpreted him and assumed an interest that wasn't there?

She stood there, turning over her thoughts, until the hot water ran out. Then she stepped out of the shower and energetically toweled herself off until her skin glowed.

Tomorrow she would go up to the cabin. There they would meet again.

"Your phone rang twice!" Nisse called from the laundry room as she came downstairs.

"Okay. Thanks."

She went up to the hall table where she had left her phone. Two missed calls, one of which was from Elliot. She would call him immediately after she talked to Göran, her boss, who had also tried to reach her.

Göran answered on the first ring.

"Hi, Embla! Are you hunting wood nymphs up there in the primeval forest?"

"Wood what?"

"Just kidding. The strand of hair you sent over was unusually long, so I told Hampus you were off hunting witches in the forest. Anyway, it is human hair. Originally it was black but it's been bleached and dyed. Sturdy, probably Indo-European. It most likely comes from a wig."

"I could have guessed as much."

"So you want to tell me what is this about?"

She hesitated for a moment. "Well . . . to be honest I don't really know. An extremely strange thing happened . . . but I'll tell you about it when I'm back."

"Okay. See you in ten days. I'll bake something good."

He knew very well that she never ate any of his cookies, but the consideration warmed her heart. *My mom, Göran*, she thought. It was a shame he was still single after the divorce; Embla wished he would at least try to meet a new woman. After his youngest son moved away from home last year to study in Luleå, it was as if he had adopted her and Hampus. He truly cared about them. At the same time he was a very competent policeman and the best boss she could ask for. She'd had unbelievable luck getting the position at VGM.

Elliot had lots to talk about. He was naturally most interested in the moose she had shot. Next year he wanted—no, he *demanded*—to go with her on the moose hunt. She didn't have the energy to argue with him, but instead simply cowardly mumbled that they would have to see then. Carefully she guided the conversation onto different paths.

"What do you think we should do when we get together next time?"

"Go to a concert! Iron Maiden!"

"Oh boy. Heavy metal. What does Jason say about that?"

"I can like whatever I want!"

"Absolutely. But have you ever really listened to Iron Maiden?"

There was silence for a moment before he finally answered. "No. Maybe not. But a guy in fourth grade has a really cool T-shirt with them on it. His dad bought it. I want a shirt like that too. But they only sell them at their shows."

"Okay. I understand. Hold on a sec." She did a quick search on her phone. "It looks like there won't be any Iron Maiden concerts in Gothenburg for a while, but I can try to get you a shirt like that."

"Great! I want one with a skull."

"I'm not promising anything, but I'll do some digging online. So what do you want to do instead?"

"Go to Lerum's water park."

"Then that's what we'll do."

She became aware that she had been smiling for a long time after she ended the call with Elliot. She had to admit it: he was the man in her life.

The rest of the day they devoted to stocking up on food for the weekend, doing laundry, and a thorough gun cleaning. At lunch, which consisted of potato pancakes with lingonberry jam and crisply fried pork, Nisse said, "Ingela really wants us to come over to her place for dinner tonight. What do you think?"

"That would be great!"

"Okay, then I'll call her and say yes."

Before they left for Ingela Gustavsson's, Embla picked a big bouquet of red and blue fall asters from Nisse's garden. Those were the only flowers still blooming that were at all beautiful, given the cold snap during the week. A few more cold nights and they would also start to look decayed. They would have to do.

The house was a traditional red wooden Swedish house. They went up the neatly raked gravel path and knocked on the door. Embla heard footsteps at once and the door opened.

"Welcome!"

Ingela was rather short and a little plump, with light, curly hair and lively blue eyes behind a pair of red eyeglass frames. Besides glowing red lip gloss she used no makeup. The silk blouse she wore was white with narrow blue stripes in the same shade as her pants. And she knew the art of walking elegantly in her red high-heeled shoes.

They stepped into the hall and hung up their jackets. Happily chatting, Ingela showed them into the kitchen. It was easy to see that she and Nisse did not have the same taste where kitchens were concerned. Hers was new, with smooth, light oak cupboard doors. There were handwoven rag rugs on the floor. All the appliances were new and of the latest model, including the induction cooktop and hot-air oven. The kitchen windows were filled with plants and the white curtain valances were hand-embroidered with flowery garlands.

Whatever was in the oven smelled good. Given the hint of cinnamon that was floating in the air, Embla guessed it must be a dessert.

On the kitchen counter their hostess had set out a small tray with three tall wine glasses. She traipsed over to the refrigerator and took out a bottle with gold foil around the cork.

"Would you like a glass of bubbly before dinner?"

Both her guests said yes. Ingela invited them to relax on the sofas in the living room, and she would join them with the wine and some snacks.

The oak parquet floor and eggshell-white walls made the room light and cozy. In front of the open fireplace were two light-blue sofas facing each other. They sat down on the sofas and soon the hostess came with champagne glasses and some snack bowls on a tray. Ingela's toast was a little solemn, but the mood quickly brightened and they talked happily about all kinds of things. Ingela was especially interested in Embla's job in the mobile unit and asked lots of questions.

After a while they brought up this year's moose hunt, and once again Embla had an opportunity to talk about the moment she felled her magnificent animal. They also talked about how the others had done and gossiped a little about the members of Anders von Beehn's hunting party. Ingela thought Embla's description of Greger Liljon's English hunting outfit was particularly amusing; she laughed heartily for a long time. While she dried the tears from her eyes she asked how things had gone for Peter.

Embla was completely caught off guard and became tongue-tied. Fortunately Nisse answered without showing the slightest surprise.

"It went fine. He shot a yearling. Really nice shot." With a faint smile he turned toward his niece. "Ingela is related to Peter," he said.

"Although distantly," Ingela interjected.

If she had noticed Embla's reaction she did not show it in any way.

"What are you? Second cousins?" Nisse asked.

"No. My grandmother and Peter's grandfather were cousins. So I guess we're third cousins."

Darned Nisse hadn't warned her in advance! But on the bright side, this was a golden opportunity to finally get more information about Peter and his family. Although Embla knew it was crucial not to appear too curious.

"So did you know Peter's father?" she asked in her best neutral tone.

"No, not that well. He was fourteen or fifteen years older."

"I've heard that something tragic happened . . ."

Before Ingela answered she gave Embla a searching look. "Yes . . . several sad things actually. First of course there was the boy's death. I think that was what started it all . . ."

Embla felt confused and started to wonder if they were talking about the same family.

"The boy's death?" Nisse asked, echoing her thoughts.

"The little boy . . . no, let's take it from the beginning. So Sven met Henrietta down in Gothenburg. They got married when she was pregnant with Camilla. Three years later a little boy was born. But it turned out that he had a severe heart defect. He only lived a few days. After that . . . it started."

A timer rang out in the kitchen and Ingela excused herself and stood up.

"Why didn't you say anything?" Embla whispered.

"I wanted to see if it was possible to start talking about Peter and his family in a natural way. And then she started to ask about him and I got stuck . . ."

He stopped talking when Ingela came into the room again.

"You can come to the table now!" she said.

The table was beautifully set with a white linen tablecloth and folded blue napkins. She had put the fall asters in a large cut crystal vase.

They had fried perch filet with pureed garlic potatoes and warm salmon roe sauce. Ingela also served lightly steamed sugar peas that she had grown herself in her garden. Dessert was a crisp apple cake with ice-cold vanilla sauce. It was as if they had a silent agreement not to pick up the conversation about the Hansson family during the meal.

They had coffee out on the blue sofas. Nisse made a new fire in the stove. Soon the fire was crackling again.

When she filled the cups and passed around pralines, Ingela sat quietly for a moment before she started speaking again.

"Peter is very much like his father. Sven was also very stylish when he was young. That he would become such a . . . drunkard . . . probably no one could have imagined."

She heaved a long sigh and sipped a little of the hot coffee before she continued.

"After the boy died, Henrietta suffered from postpartum depression. Sven started drinking even more, but after a year or so he got help from the company health service. He got some kind of medicine and stopped drinking alcohol, and it seemed as if Henrietta had gotten better too. A few years passed before Peter was born. Outwardly everything seemed to be as it should, but . . ." Ingela interrupted herself again and pressed her lips together.

"So you mean there were things that weren't so good?" Nisse interjected.

He would have been an excellent interview leader, thought Embla. *I take after him in so many ways.*

"Well . . . there were rumors. Henrietta was . . . silent. Peter was a taciturn boy who mostly kept to himself." Once again she sighed and drank the last of her coffee, which had now become lukewarm.

"I'll go out and get more coffee," Nisse offered.

When all three had their refills, Embla asked, "What was his sister, Camilla, like?"

"She was a lot younger so I didn't know her. But people did talk . . . afterward . . . when she disappeared. When she was little she was rather demure, but in high school there were problems. She started going out with boys and riding around in hot rods. Normal teenage defiance, of course. But she developed into a real beauty. The boys chased her. Then she started at the high school in Åmål and got involved with an older boy. There was a lot of . . .

arguing . . . between her and Sven. No one seemed to be particularly surprised when she disappeared. Everyone assumed she'd had enough and ran away. But over the years I've often wondered what really happened. It's been thirty years now and not the slightest sign of life has turned up."

"So Camilla disappeared. Tell me how that happened," Embla carefully encouraged her.

Ingela watched the flames dance behind the sooty glass cover of the wood stove for a few moments before she continued her story. "Camilla and her boyfriend were at a party with one of his friends, who lived about twenty kilometers from here. She had strict orders to be home before one A.M. But when it was time to go home, her boyfriend was dead drunk and couldn't drive. They started arguing. Because Camilla had the Hansson temperament she pulled on her jacket and stormed out of the house. That was the last time anyone saw her."

There was silence for a while. The fire crackled cozily and spread a lovely warmth in the room, but Embla was shivering. Peter had a number of heavy things in his baggage.

"I assume there was a search for her," Embla said.

"Of course. Lots of tips came in, but nothing that led to anything. It was an awful time. Especially for the family. It divided them."

There were many pieces in Ingela's story that fell into place in the complicated puzzle around Peter.

Embla had to ask the question that constantly came up: "Why do you think that Peter came back here?"

"To be honest I've wondered that myself, but I have no idea. It's odd. He doesn't really know anyone here, and he doesn't seem to be doing anything to change that. He keeps to himself for the most part."

The fire started to die down and the shadows in the corners deepened. Ingela got up from the sofa and went up to the stove to add more wood to the fire. Then she turned around and remained standing with her back to the stove.

"Because Camilla was never found, dead nor alive, most people thought she managed to get a lift with someone to Gothenburg. That's what I heard. Over the years the story faded into obscurity and nothing happened. Until Sven died and Peter returned."

When Ingela returned to the sofa, she looked a bit mournful.

They left the subject of the Hansson family's tragic history and talked about other things for another hour or so, before Embla said it was time to go. Even though they had already loaded the car, they had to get up no later than four-thirty to make it up to the hunting cabin. At seven o'clock sharp they should be sitting at their stations.

ON THE WAY to the hunt the next morning, Sixten and Nisse were napping in the backseat of the Jeep. Between them lay Seppo, who was snoring the loudest. Embla and Björn sat in the front seat, but didn't say much so as not to disturb the old men.

As the Jeep turned onto the yard in front of the cabins, the headlights swept over Tobias and Einar. They were standing next to their big vehicle, talking to a man who was also dressed in hunting clothes. When they got closer, Embla saw that it was the manager, Stig Ekström.

"Hello there! Up already?" Björn called heartily as he got out of the Jeep.

None of the men said anything or flashed a smile. All three looked dead serious.

"Has something happened?" Nisse asked.

All of his previous tiredness suddenly disappeared and his voice sounded clear and sharp.

"Don't know. Stig just arrived. Tell them," said Einar.

Nisse looked urgently at the manager. Stig Ekström was a rather taciturn person who kept a low profile. Now he stood, squirming self-consciously.

"I can't find them," he said quietly.

"Who?" Nisse asked.

"Von Beehn and Cahneborg. They're . . . gone."

"They're not in the house?"

"No. Not outside either."

There was silence for a while as everyone wondered whether this was a problem or something that could have a completely reasonable explanation.

Embla looked around. Peter wasn't there either, she noticed. But maybe he had decided he was done hunting for the week, especially considering the unsatisfactory way the two of them had left things. "When did you last see them?" she asked the group after a while.

"On Wednesday evening. I was off on Thursday."

"And you didn't come up here yesterday either?"

"No. Before I left Anders said they needed to take a day off. Relax. They had enough food. I didn't need to come until today."

The information was again followed by silence.

"That's damned peculiar! They usually hunt every day they're here," Tobias pointed out.

Stig Ekström shrugged his shoulders but did not reply.

"Yes, I can't recall them ever taking a break during the hunt. They usually take advantage of the time," said Einar.

The others mumbled in agreement. Embla thought of an important question.

"Is the car still here?"

"Yes. It hasn't been moved."

"So where the hell are they?" Sixten asked.

Now he also seemed wide-awake.

"I guess we'll have to find that out," said Embla.

Everyone fell silent when they heard the sound of an engine approaching. Then the lights from a car danced between the tree trunks as Peter's Range Rover turned onto the yard. He braked and was out of the car almost before it had stopped. With long strides he paced up to them.

"Excuse me for being late. I overslept," he said.

He blinked toward the light from the flashlights that were aimed at him and stopped. His coarsely knit blue wool sweater matched his worn blue jeans and suited him perfectly.

Fresh and sexy, thought Embla. Then she felt the surge in her abdomen. Damn, this was serious. "Tell him," she said, poking Nisse in the side with her elbow.

THE DARKNESS WAS still dense as the group walked toward the Hunting Castle. Nisse let Seppo run around on the full extension of the retractable leash. The dog was still sleepy and only nosed around distractedly, dutifully peeing a few squirts from time to time to let the game in the forest know that he was back. He appeared to be comfortable with Tilly, who plodded along at Einar's side.

The wind had picked up during the morning hours and the air chapped their faces. At any moment the rain could turn to ice or sleet could start falling. If everything had been as usual they would have been sitting indoors having a good breakfast, but that would have to wait. The highest priority was finding Anders von Beehn and Jan-Eric Cahneborg.

Perched on the rise above the lake, the Hunting Castle was submerged in darkness, with only one outdoor light on a corner of the house turned on. A short distance away they could see that the lantern by the precipice was also shining. It was almost six-thirty but the dense clouds were blocking any sign of dawn.

Embla turned toward Stig Ekström. "Was the door to the Hunting Castle locked when you arrived?" she asked.

The manager looked nervous. "It was open. But closed," he answered, confused.

"Unlocked, you mean. Was there a fire in the stove?" she continued.

"No. It was cold in the house."

"And you've searched all through the place? The cellar too?"

"Everywhere. The cellar is just a little food cellar. There's nothing there."

"Did they take the guns with them?"

"I didn't think to check," Ekström said.

"Then let's do that. Stig and I will go into the house. We'll check the outbuilding, too. Nisse and Seppo, you go around the lake. Sixten, Peter, and Björn will search in the other direction. Toby . . ."

"Who put you in charge?" Sixten interrupted her.

He was evidently not pleased by the thought of stumbling around in the dark in the company of Peter, even if Björn was with them. Besides, he was the hunting leader and was used to being the one who told people where they should be and in whose company. His entire body language radiated that no little snip of a girl would come here and boss the guys around just like that.

"I've done this many times in my line of work," Embla cut him off.

That silenced him for the moment.

"You can come with me, if you want," Nisse offered.

Sixten grunted something that was evidently supposed to represent a yes.

"Tobias and Einar, bring Tilly with you and take a closer look at the old butchering shed," Embla continued.

"Is there anything left of it?" Einar asked.

"And what the hell would the guys do in that old shack?" his son objected.

"I don't know. But it's there. Every conceivable place has to be searched."

She wondered whether there was anything she had forgotten. There probably was, but that would have to be sorted out during the organized search.

STIG EKSTRÖM TURNED on the switch in the hall as they stepped inside. The air felt cold and raw; apparently there had been no fire in the big fireplace in the main room for a while.

"We'll start with the bedrooms," Embla decided.

They went up the creaking stairs to the top floor, which she had never seen before. The air felt raw and the small stoves in the bedrooms were also cold. The temperature was set to ten degrees Celsius and it was no more than that in the house.

When they opened the door to Anders von Beehn's bedroom, slightly warmer air streamed toward them. She checked the thermostat in the room and saw that it was set at eighteen degrees.

The dominant piece of furniture in the room was an extra-wide bed. The cover was wrinkled as if someone had been lying on top of it and hadn't smoothed it out afterward. Some pillows were set up against the headboard. A folded pair of glasses rested on an open book on the nightstand. The other furniture consisted of a wardrobe, a wicker basket equipped with a lock, and a rug with a Persian pattern that looked old and worn. A sturdy dresser beside the window appeared to be of a respectable age. On top of it was a gold watch, a crocodile skin wallet, and an iPhone. She tried to turn on the phone. Dead.

The things on the dresser worried her. They could mean that von Beehn had not intended to go very far from the house. Carefully she picked up the wallet and looked in it. It was without a doubt Anders von Beehn's; she found his driver's license in a transparent plastic pocket.

There were four five-hundred-kronor bills inside, as well as several credit and debit cards.

Nothing in the room indicated a struggle. Everything looked tidy.

"Do you see anything that's missing from the room or that looks strange?"

Stig Ekström looked around carefully but then shook his head. "No. But I'm seldom on the top floor during the hunt. Anna and I get the rooms ready before the guests arrive, and we clean when they've gone home."

"Where does Anders store his guns?"

"Here." He went up to a wallpapered door that was recessed in the wall. She hadn't noticed it until he pulled on a little knob and the door opened. The closet was small. He had to crouch when he stepped in and turn on the flashlight to see anything. "His Carl Gustaf is missing," he said.

"That's the rifle he uses during the moose hunt."

"Yes. But his hunting vest is hanging here."

"Really? So what does he have on?"

"Probably his gray wool sweater. With a crocodile mark on the chest. He usually wears it indoors. But I'll take a look in the wardrobe."

He went up to the large wardrobe and opened the door. Inside were neat piles of clean underwear and socks on the side shelves. Two pairs of pants and two jackets were on hangers, one a bit lighter and one of sturdy tweed. Three ironed shirts were also hanging up, but there was no gray Lacoste-brand sweater.

Ekström raised the lid of the round woven-wicker laundry basket. "The laundry," he said.

"Do you usually take it with you when you drive back to Dalsnäs?"

"Yes, but not every day. Although on Wednesday I took a load with me."

Embla also went up to the basket and looked down into it. All that was on the bottom was a pair of black men's socks and a pair of underwear: the dirty laundry from Thursday's deer hunt. There was nothing from Friday. It was not a good sign, but she didn't say that out loud. Instead she asked, "Where does he keep his hunting clothes?"

"Downstairs. Hanging in the hall by the kitchen entrance. All the hunters usually hang their clothes there after they're done. There's a drying cupboard and such if that's needed. And shoe dryers."

Slightly higher accommodations than our cabin, she thought, pursing her lips slightly.

They went to Jan-Eric Cahneborg's room, which was farther down the corridor. The rooms between them were empty when they looked in. Stig told her he had cleaned them out already on Wednesday afternoon. The attorney Lennart Folkesson had stayed in one, and Volker Heinz had stayed in the adjacent room. Greger Liljon had stayed in the smallest room at the far end of the corridor.

It was also warm in Cahneborg's room, and it was a glorious mess in there. To be fair, the room was somewhat smaller than von Beehn's, but clothes and things were spread out all over. The closet door was wide open and a pair of jeans was hanging over the closet rod, along with a soiled shirt and a pair of suit pants. The matching jacket was draped over the back of a chair. Almost hidden under dirty underwear, undershirts, and socks that littered the floor was an empty bottle of whiskey. But the bottle on the nightstand was half full. *Or half empty, if you were more pessimistically inclined*, thought Embla. Two rifle cases were leaning in one corner of the closet.

"Does it usually look this way in Jan-Eric's room?" she asked.

"Yes . . . most of the time."

It was unbelievable that a grown man could make such a mess. He must be used to having others pick up after him, Embla assumed.

"Does von Beehn usually drink a lot during the hunts, too?"

"No. I've never seen him drunk."

"But Cahneborg is not someone who's shy when there's alcohol," she said, pointing at the bottles.

That was not a question, but a statement. The manager grunted something that could be interpreted as agreement. She went over to the closet and picked up the rifle cases. They were heavy; there were rifles in both of them.

"Do you know if he had more than two guns with him?"

He simply shrugged his shoulders in response.

Embla opened the cases and looked more closely at the rifles. One was the gun he usually had at the moose hunts, a caliber 30-06 Carl Gustaf. Naturally she took the opportunity to look more closely at the other rifle, too. It was double-barreled. It must have cost a fortune. The stock was artfully decorated with gold inlays and what looked like ivory. Illegal, but a very fine gun, she had to admit that. Reluctantly she put the rifle back in the case.

As a matter of form they searched through the three remaining bedrooms before they went down to the ground floor.

The kitchen was large and well-equipped, but clearly only breakfast was prepared there. The refrigerator was full of food, white wine, and beer. In the pantry were several unopened bottles of red wine and various kinds of alcohol.

With some effort Stig opened a hatch in the floor and peeked down in the hole. "The food cellar."

They shined the flashlights down into the hole, simply to determine that there were only a lot of empty bottles and strangely active spiders. The webs were hanging like drapes all over the space.

"It's never used," Stig explained, somewhat superfluously.

"I can see why." Embla shivered as she said that. Big spiders were the only creatures she couldn't stand. Especially furry ones.

Then they checked the hall behind the kitchen, where the hunting clothes were hanging. Stig explained to Embla that he could see that Anders's and Jan-Eric's boots were missing, but that their jackets were still hanging there.

"They've gone out but haven't put on their jackets. So they didn't intend to go very far," she said.

"Hardly in the darkness."

"How do you know that it was dark?"

"Two flashlights are missing." He pointed at a shelf by the door where six flashlights were neatly lined up. "There are usually eight there."

Most signs indicated that they had disappeared on Thursday evening. The sparse quantity of dirty laundry at the bottom of the laundry basket suggested that, as well as the cold in the house. And there was a lot of food left in the kitchen.

Her thoughts were interrupted when the two-way radio suddenly crackled.

"Nisse here. Seppo . . . has got a lead on something. He swam out to the drop and refuses to come back. It seems like . . . there's something in the water. But you need a boat to get out there. Over and out!"

For once his voice sounded unsteady.

"Embla here. Stay there! We're coming. Over and out." She turned toward the manager.

"There's a rubber boat in the shed," he said before she had time to ask.

They turned on their flashlights and ran out into the rain. When they got to the shed Stig took out a key from a bulky key ring. After some coaxing he managed to get the stubborn padlock open. He let the beam of his flashlight play across the room. Old tools and gardening equipment were hanging on the walls, along with a bundle of fishing rods and some broken crayfish pots. A single battered piece of outdoor furniture was in the middle of the floor, and there was a large, lumpy sack in one corner.

"I cleaned this place up a little when I sealed the house against mice. I saw it then," said Stig.

With long strides he went over to the bundle in the corner and started pulling it toward the door. With combined forces they managed to compress the nylon sack enough to squeeze it through the door.

Stig stuck his head back in the doorway and shined around his flashlight. "Anders and his buddies used the boat to catch crayfish. There should be an automatic gadget to inflate it . . . although I don't see it in here . . ."

They quickly searched through the outbuilding but didn't see anything that resembled a pump. Working together they managed to pull off the bag that surrounded the rubber boat. Both sighed with relief when the pump and two paddles tumbled to the ground.

The grass was slippery with rain and they fell a few times as they struggled to get the boat in the back of the car. Before they closed the hatch Embla threw in a rope that she had taken down from a hook on the wall.

A sickly yellow-gray light started to cut through the darkness.

"The worst remains," Ekström said with a sigh.

"What do you mean?"

"There's no road down to the water."

"But this vehicle is off-road, damn it!"

Her voice sounded much sharper than she intended,

but she got irritated when people complained a lot. They would have to work through the difficulties gradually and not get ahead of themselves. Without answering Stig got into the driver's seat of the King Cab. He chose to drive to the left of the precipice. That was the way you usually took when you went down to the lake to fish or swim. It was obvious that no car had ever driven that route before and there was no doubt about why. The heavy vehicle lurched and rocked; sometimes it felt as if it would flip over.

When they stopped by the lake, properly shaken, they saw Nisse and Sixten squatting in the rain a short distance away. Nisse called to Seppo, but the dog only raised his nose toward the sky and howled in response. He was at the foot of the drop where there was a narrow strip of beach with large stones. With his back to them he sat motionless on the biggest stone, staring at something in the shallow water.

It was surprisingly easy to inflate the rubber boat. You only had to put the mouthpiece of the pump into the hole and press a button.

Before long Embla and Nisse paddled off. The rain poured down and felt just as cold as the lake water. It did not take long before their fingers were stiff and numb. As they got closer they saw there was a person lying below the drop. Judging by the shape of the body it was Jan-Eric Cahneborg. He was lying face down in the shallow water. One arm had been wedged firmly between two stones and was bent at a strange angle.

The dog got lively when he saw that they were headed in his direction. Excitedly he started barking.

"Yes, yes, calm down. That's a good boy. Swim in now so we can take care of this," Nisse said to his dog.

Seppo fell silent as if he understood what his master said, jumped down into the water and started swimming toward the shore. Thinking ahead, Embla pulled out her cell phone and took a few pictures of the body from different angles—just in case. In case of what, well, she didn't want to think about that just yet. Just as the dog reached land, Peter and Björn came up to the lake, and a few minutes later Tobias and Einar arrived. Silently the men stood and watched as Nisse and Embla struggled to get Jan-Eric's arm loose. Once they succeeded, it was just a matter of piloting the body to shore. It was difficult to move in the unsteady craft, and the boat nearly capsized several times, but after a while they managed to throw the rope around the torso. Nisse tied the other end around his own waist since there was nothing else in the rubber boat to attach it to. When that was done they started slowly rowing to shore.

When they were almost there, Sixten shouted, "Which of them is it?"

"Cahneborg," Embla answered.

"You saw no trace of the other one out there?"

"No. We'll have to keep searching. But first I intend to call for reinforcements."

In order to get cell phone coverage Embla was forced to climb the steep slope. Alongside the lantern by the edge of the precipice she was able to get two bars at least.

At first the on-duty commander in Trollhättan was extremely doubtful that any crime scene investigators were needed since it sounded like an accidental fall. A man was peeing in the dark, slipped on a wet rock, and fell down the precipice . . . no, he didn't think that sounded like a situation for a crime scene investigation. But Embla stood her ground and told him about Anders von Beehn's mysterious disappearance. She emphasized the fact that the two men were well-known and influential in the world of finance, and she could hear the commander start to waver. After a little more convincing he gave in and promised to send CSIs and a patrol car.

While they were waiting for the police the search for Anders von Beehn continued. Embla underscored that he was armed, and because they didn't know what had played out between the two men, they should have that information in the back of their minds.

The men divided into pairs and went in different

directions to resume the search. Both of the dogs they had with them were good at searching. Embla chose to stay by the lake. It was clear that none of the men relished the thought of watching over a corpse alone. She could see their point; it wasn't much fun to stand idle in the semi-darkness, trying to protect yourself against the damp and cold.

The only positive thing that happened was that the rain stopped after a while, but the dense cloud cover remained and prevented more light from shining through.

Jan-Eric's head shimmered like white marble in the gloom and the rigor mortis started to disappear. That confirmed her suspicion that he had already fallen down the precipice on Thursday evening or night. She noted that his fly was open, which supported the theory that he slipped as he was pissing into the darkness. He had no jacket on, only a thick green wool sweater with a short zipper on the collar. His boots were untied. Maybe he had stumbled on the laces.

It felt frustrating not to have anything to cover the body with, but she decided to let it be. Later she could go up to the house and find a blanket.

She did not want to move the corpse again; she would leave that to the medical examiners. When she had concluded her visual inspection, she climbed back up the steep slope. There she took out her phone and called her boss, Göran Krantz. After several rings he answered, and she could hear the sound of a TV in the background.

"Hi. It's me. Where are you?" she asked.

"At home. But I'm probably the one who should ask where you are," he answered good-naturedly.

She took a deep breath and told him the whole story

about what had played out during the morning hours. The superintendent did not interrupt her a single time.

"Can von Beehn be behind Cahneborg's death?" he asked when she was done.

"I haven't seen or found anything that indicates that they were enemies. But I thought of something out here in the middle of nowhere with the corpse. There is one more dead friend."

Göran Krantz was silent for a fraction of a second before he exploded. "One more! Who? Where is he?"

"Probably in a cemetery in Oslo. He died almost exactly one year ago. And here comes the bombshell: he drove off the road when he was going home after the moose hunt here. I know because I was on that hunt. And he was friends with Anders von Beehn. Just like Cahneborg."

"Hmm. What's the guy's name?"

"Ola Forsnaess. He was big in the oil industry, I think."

After a moment of thoughtful silence he asked, "What do you intend to do now?"

"Wait for reinforcements. Colleagues from Trollhättan are on their way."

"Good. Be careful. This actually sounds serious."

As she put the phone back in the front pocket of her jacket she looked at the body down by the edge of the lake. It looked pitiful there alone. Very cold and dead, she thought with a shudder.

She jumped when she suddenly heard a faint squelching of footsteps approaching her from behind. Realizing she was barely a meter from the edge of the drop, she spun around with lightning speed, her fists ready in defense.

"Oh! I didn't mean to scare you."

Peter took a step backward and raised his hands in a defensive gesture. When she saw that it was him she didn't know if she was relieved or enraged.

"No? You have one hell of a talent for sneaking up on people!" she snarled.

He bowed his head and looked down at the ground. He cleared his throat several times before he raised his head and looked at her with a steady gaze. "Listen, I want to apologize for my behavior toward you yesterday morning. That was not okay. I've been stressed about the big transaction I negotiated. And I'm so fucking tired of all the bullshit that's being spread about me in the area. It felt like you had been sent to spy on me . . . paranoid, I know. But when you work with highly classified material all the time you get occupationally injured."

She didn't know how to respond. In truth, she actually had been out to snoop, but she wasn't about to admit it. Instead she tried to collect herself and answer as naturally as possible.

"I can see that. And if it hadn't been for the Veteran running out of gas, I wouldn't have come and disturbed you."

"But I wanted to be disturbed by you," he said with a faint smile.

She did her best to seem unmoved but knew she wasn't doing a good job of that. "Yes?" was the only thing she got out.

His smile got broader. "We didn't get off on the right foot. I think we should start over. What do you say about dinner tomorrow night?"

What a completely absurd situation. Here they were, two people in the middle of the woods with a dead person a few feet away and another man missing. And yet . . .

she felt herself getting warm all over. But that was not something her more reasonable self intended to show because she too was occupationally injured.

"We'll have to see if we find Anders," she answered curtly.

"Okay. We'll see what tomorrow brings."

He turned and started walking toward the Hunting Castle. Before she thought to ask what he was going to do in the house, he looked back and said over his shoulder, "We're about to starve to death. No one's had a real breakfast. I'll make coffee and some sandwiches. Stig said that everything is in the kitchen. The others will be here before long."

"Okay. Sounds good. I'll try to find something to put over the body. It may take a while before the technicians arrive."

She thought about the case for the rubber boat that was still lying outside the shed. Perhaps that would do the job.

The first three police officers who had been dispatched got stuck in the mud on the logging road, so Tobias went out with his pickup and towed them. A few minutes later two CSIs came in a Volvo Cross Country, which could easily make it all the way.

The police from Trollhättan joined the group of hunters inside the big hall of the Hunting Castle. Stig Ekström had lit a fire in the stove to try to warm up the house. While the five colleagues had coffee and sandwiches, Embla recapped the morning's events.

The commander introduced himself as Superintendent Roger Willén. He was just over forty and appeared to be in decent shape. His uniform sat well across his broad shoulders and the crease in his trousers was razor sharp. His hair was cut so short that it was impossible to say what color it was. Willén looked thoughtfully around the table before he continued to speak.

"So you started searching for these two men at about six o'clock this morning. That guy in the lake . . . Canne . . . Cahneborg, yes . . . you found him around eight. It took a while to recover the body and then you called us," he said, nodding toward Embla.

"Yes," she answered.

It felt good to have some colleagues to reinforce the group. Besides, it was surely a relief for Sixten that a male authority took over, she thought.

"It's almost eleven. Because Anders von . . . what was his name again? . . . thanks . . . Beehn hasn't moved his car. He ought to be around here. But you've already been searching for several hours. You suspect he's lying injured or unconscious out in the woods, or in the worst case, dead or on the run. Time is an important factor in these kinds of cases and for that reason I intend to call for more men. Unfortunately right now we're short-staffed because we had a homicide last weekend, but we'll request reinforcements from the rest of Fyrbodal. But it's going to take at least two hours before anyone else can get here and it gets dark quickly."

"Perhaps you can call for a helicopter with a heat camera." Peter suggested.

Superintendent Willén looked at him seriously and hesitated with the answer. "You can't just order a helicopter; it costs lots of money. But I'll do what I can to get one here."

After that he sent them off in various directions with strict instructions to maintain contact with each other.

AT TWO O'CLOCK a group of volunteer national guardsmen arrived, along with two police officers from Åmål. An appeal on Facebook to Missing People had not produced any results yet. Perhaps reinforcements would come from that group tomorrow, but Embla knew that was not something they could count on. There was no major metropolitan area nearby.

It had started to rain again but everyone was properly clothed. They walked in tight ranks with short gaps and poked their staffs into thickets and used them to feel the bottom of creeks and puddles.

The only result was that the game in the area got upset and started wandering around. Seppo was overjoyed when he managed to chase a wild boar out of its den. He was also the only one who was satisfied with the results of the search.

They found no trace of Anders von Beehn.

WHEN THE ORGANIZED search was called off it had been dark for several hours and Roger Willén was noticeably dejected, but he tried to conceal it under a professional surface.

"A fresh group of guys from the national guard is coming who will continue to search during the night. If they don't find von Beehn, we'll have to call in a helicopter with heat camera and divers who can search in the lake. We'll gather here at seven o'clock tomorrow morning," he said.

After that he thanked everyone for their commitment and then turned toward Embla.

"Can we talk?"

"Of course."

They went into the Hunting Castle and sat down by the open fireplace. The fire had gone out, but the stones were still lukewarm. It was the warmest place they could find. Ten degrees above freezing inside was better than the damp, freezing-point air outside, but neither of them shed any layers of clothing. It was crucial to retain the warmth you managed to generate. Embla felt both hungry and cold.

"You know everyone involved and you've been here for the entire hunt and seen everything that's happened the past few days. It would be helpful if you wrote a report about what's been going on," Roger Willén said, getting right to the point.

At first she was completely speechless. Perhaps her low blood sugar was affecting her; she felt anger welling up inside her.

"Listen, I'm on vacation. It's your job to write a report. No way am I going to do it!" She met his glance and noticed he was perplexed. "I'm a detective inspector. Not your secretary!" she added while she still had her dander up.

Willén swallowed several times. "I thought that perhaps you would be a little collegial," he said stiffly.

"Collegial! I've been collegial since six o'clock this morning! I was the one who organized the search and found Jan-Eric. I was the one who paddled out and retrieved him. I called you and—"

"Thanks. Forget I asked."

They glared at each other but both were too tired to keep up a longer staring contest.

The superintendent took a deep breath. "If we just have you record everything would that work?"

She quickly made an assessment. She was aware that she let her temper take over. Obviously it was best to have good relationships with her colleagues. It didn't hurt to show a little willingness to cooperate.

"What do you want me to do?" she asked.

"Record yourself telling me the story—anything you think is important. And anything else, too, for that matter. Just so we can get a picture of the course of events."

Yes, she could actually take that on. But there was a hitch.

"I don't have a tape recorder."

"We do. A little mini-recorder."

"Okay. Then I'll record it this evening. I also have some photos I took on my phone before we moved the body. They're not great quality, but I'll send them to you."

"Thanks. That will be a great help."

It sounded as if he meant that.

THE SEARCH TEAM reconvened at the Hunting Castle as agreed at seven o'clock the next morning. Before they went out in the woods, Embla handed the recording to Superintendent Willén. She had recorded it after Nisse and Björn had gone to bed. If you listened carefully you could hear Nisse's snoring in the background. In any case she thought she did.

The search continued like the day before, with the hacking sound from a helicopter in the air above.

The divers had also arrived in their specially equipped van. The lake was not large; their commander thought they would be done during the day. A new group of soldiers would arrive late in the morning and hopefully a number of volunteers would come from Missing People as well.

WHEN THE SEARCH was called off late that evening, they still had not found the slightest trace of Anders von Beehn.

The hunting party gathered again by the cabins where they all agreed to go home for the night. Everyone felt a strong need to shower and get some sleep in their regular beds.

EMBLA PARKED HER old car in front of Hansgården. The entire farmyard was bathed in light. The thought popped up again: *Who is he afraid of?* But maybe it was like he said and the material he worked with would be very attractive to competing companies and criminals who dealt in industrial espionage. It was strange though. Didn't the thefts of IT secrets usually happen, for obvious reasons, on the Internet?

She firmly dismissed all thoughts of crime in cyberspace and decided to try to relax and have a pleasant evening. Now that she knew more about Peter's background she could better understand why he was guarded with other people. Hopefully he would change his attitude when they got to know each other a little better.

As she ran her hand over her newly washed hair, she felt it was still damp. She wore it loose, so it would soon be dry. Once again she had put on her good sweater, leaving her left shoulder bare. With the sweater, she wore a pair of tight jeans. She had done laundry the day before and with a few sprays of perfume in strategic places she smelled good. Most of all it was nice to exchange the rubber hunting boots for a pair of light ankle boots.

The front door opened before she could knock. Peter

welcomed her with a radiant smile and a warm hug. He took the opportunity to give her a light kiss on the cheek, close to the corner of her mouth. It didn't feel overly intimate, but a thrill passed through her body. She wanted more of that. He courteously took her jacket and hung it up in the closet. Then he put his arm around her waist and guided her into the living room, where the lighting was subdued. There were candles all over in low glass holders. The candles in the chandelier over the coffee table were also lit, and the glow from the flames reflected off the shiny marble surface. A silver wine cooler and two tall glasses glistened on the little table between the chairs in front of the wood stove. Behind the glass doors of the stove the flames crackled.

She gasped for breath. "You've really gone all out!" she said as she exhaled.

A smile gleamed in his eyes. "You have to if you're trying to repair a bad impression."

He invited her to sit down and took the bottle out of the cooler, wrapped a cloth napkin around it, and opened the cork with a pop. A glance at the label showed that it was genuine champagne.

"Fair warning: I'm going to pass out after one glass," she said.

That was no exaggeration, she felt drained in both body and soul after two long days of fruitless searching. There had also been the lack of sleep.

"The same goes for me, so since I think it's safe to assume this bottle will be enough, I've gone for a better brand," he said with a wink. He filled the glasses and handed her one.

As she took it he caught her gaze. Her heart skipped a beat, and she sincerely hoped that it didn't show that she was blushing. To hide her nerves she said, "I can feel it in my feet. I've been moving all the time for two days. Normally we just sit at our stations for the most part."

"You feel stiff, too."

That was a statement. His smile became more devious and there was a mischievous gleam in his eyes.

"Stiff, yes. And yet I'm in pretty good shape," she said.

"Good shape . . . listen, let's make a toast. Then I'll show you something. Cheers!"

With a broad smile he raised the misted glass and again looked her deep in the eyes. Her heart fluttered again and she felt the warmth spreading in her body. A handsome man, intelligent and exciting with his little secrets. And who didn't have secrets? She liked all of it. But she didn't want to appear too eager.

When they had taken the first sip he stood up and extended his hand to her.

"Come on. Bring the glass with you. Now you'll get to see something I haven't shown you before," he said.

Without hesitating she took his outstretched hand and followed him over to the kitchen. They crossed the kitchen floor, up to a closed door. The one she didn't have time to look behind the last time she had done a house inspection. He let go of her hand and opened the door. With a proud gesture he pointed into the room and exclaimed, "Ta-da! My gym!"

She stepped in and looked around the space. Along one wall were four different pieces of exercise equipment, one of which was a decent-sized treadmill. She was very familiar with the brand. These were professional machines. In one corner he had installed a sauna with glass walls, and under the oblong window with frosted pane she saw a big Jacuzzi. Two soft, white terry-cloth bath towels were hanging on the wall. The floor was of the same beautiful granite as the rest of the house.

"Very nice!" she exclaimed.

"Thanks. I'm quite happy with it. This is the old laundry room that I've expanded. It's still behind the door over there." He pointed toward a door on the opposite wall.

"Cheers to your fine gym," she said, raising her glass.

When they had toasted he looked her steadily in the eyes. "The Jacuzzi stays at thirty-eight degrees. Care for a dip in the whirlpool? A little massage is always nice."

That thrilling wave passed through her again, but she didn't know how she should answer. She should probably play it cool.

"Absolutely!" she heard herself say.

Then they undressed each other. She set her glass on the edge of the whirlpool, but happened to bump it, and it fell in the water. But neither of them paid much attention to that. They were fully occupied with other things.

HE INVITED HER to sleep over but she declined. Talk was surely already going around the area. The Veteran was well-known here in the sticks, and the car had been parked on the illuminated farmyard at Hansgården for several hours already. Even though the farm was out of the way, someone had most likely seen it. But as she drove away, Embla had to admit to herself that she felt better than she had in a very long time.

Everything felt right with Peter. Although he had been a bit . . . short with her after her snooping, he was a totally different man now. He had warmed up to her and she to him. For once, she thought to herself with a smile, she hadn't fallen for a jerk.

EMBLA AWOKE TO sounds from down in the kitchen. As she fumbled for her phone she saw that it was already a quarter past seven. She stretched before she got up and went into the small guest bathroom. A glance in the mirror revealed a serious case of bedhead; the danger of having sex with damp hair. It was hopeless to try to brush the reluctant strands back into place. The only immediate option was to tie it all up in a bun and affix it to the top of her head with hairpins and rubber bands. After that her hairstyle was more presentable.

"Why didn't you wake me up?" she asked as she stepped into the kitchen.

Nisse was sitting at the kitchen table reading the newspaper. He looked up at her over the edge of his reading glasses. "I thought you needed to sleep in. This is supposed to resemble a vacation anyway," he answered with a wry smile.

"Well, that's fallen apart completely! But I have lots of comp time to use, so I'll come back here as soon as I can. Although it won't be for at least a month. Elliot and I are also planning to come up for a few days during fall break. Even though we can't hunt then."

"I hope it's possible to arrange that comp time. There

are a few moose left in the quota. If they haven't all run away from our area. There's a heck of a lot of disturbances in the forest right now."

"If we can just find Anders von Beehn it will be calm again."

Nisse gave her a thoughtful look. "Do you think so?"

She chose not to answer. Instead she poured yogurt and muesli into a bowl and sat down at the table. Sure, she still had stiffness in her feet and calves, but otherwise she was feeling great. The evening with Peter had been a real miracle cure. She noticed that she was smiling and quickly erased her satisfied expression.

"He must still be in the area. Dead or alive," she said quickly.

"And if he isn't?"

"Where would he go on foot? To the west there are only forests and the mountains of Norway, and to the north is the forest and lakes southwest of Årjäng. Looking east it's also completely desolate, and if he heads south he'll be here. If he goes to the southeast he may end up in Bengtsfors. It's at least fifty kilometers in any direction before you reach a populated area. And if he stumbled across some smaller place on the way we would have known about it by now."

"Not if he's staying away voluntarily," said Nisse.

"You think he could be behind Cahneborg's death?"

"It's not out of the question, is it?"

"But it looks like an accidental fall. Even if Anders did push Jan-Eric, he doesn't need to hide. There are no suspicions of homicide."

"Not yet."

Her brain was working at high speed while she filled a

tea ball with herbal tea, set it in the cup, and poured in hot water.

"But why would he do something like that? They've been friends for a really long time," she said at last.

"Well, he did say to Stig not to come back on Friday. They were supposed to take a rest day and that has never happened before. But maybe they had something important to discuss and then they had a falling out. So when Cahneborg went out to the precipice later, von Beehn pushed him down."

There could be something to that scenario, thought Embla. But there was an obvious objection: if Anders von Beehn had pushed Jan-Eric Cahneborg down the drop, he wouldn't have needed to flee. Running only made him appear guilty. He could have calmly gone back into the cabin again. There he could have kept reading his book, turned off the lamp and gone to bed. The next day naturally he would have called the police and reported his friend missing. When later on Friday morning he and Stig Ekström went to search, they would have found Cahneborg below the drop. A tragic accident.

But it hadn't turned out that way.

"We can't rule out that there was a third person up there on Thursday evening," she said at last.

"If that's so . . . then this is worse than we thought."

Embla did not contradict him. She felt an ice-cold shiver run down her spine and thought about what her grandmother Aina used to say when she shivered for no reason: "Someone is walking over my grave."

A SHORT TIME later Stig Ekström came to pick them up. Sitting beside him in the front seat was Sixten

Svensson. Now it was high time to cut up the animals that were hanging in the shed. Embla usually went along to assist and carry. It was a heavy job and all strong arms were needed. Because Sixten and Nisse were starting to get up in years, and Stig wasn't a youngster either, she was considering taking a course in butchering that winter. Nisse had already taught her a fair amount, but she wanted to be able to cut the animals up the right way. Sometimes she thought there was a little too much ground meat and pieces for stew.

As hunting leader, Sixten was responsible for dividing up the meat within the hunting party. Every year he made meticulous lists, which he called "the meat lists." If there was the slightest complaint from anyone concerning the distribution he could simply stick the lists under the nose of the dissatisfied party. Then whoever complained would usually give in.

The rain had stopped and the thermometer stood at one degree below freezing, which was excellent weather for handling raw meat.

They were only a few kilometers from the butchering shed when Embla's phone rang. On the display she saw that it was her colleague Hampus Stahre at VGM.

"What trouble have you been causing *now* out there in the wilderness?" he said in a high-pitched voice.

"Pushed a man over a precipice and hid a second so no one would ever find him," she answered quickly.

"What?"

"Just kidding. What do you want?"

Hampus regained his composure. "There's one heck of an uproar down here. Those two are real hotshots so we've been besieged by the media."

She was about to respond when she completely lost the thread. There were several cars parked outside the shed, including a big van with the Swedish Television *West News* logo.

"It seems like they've found their way here, too," she said gloomily.

As they came closer she could see Superintendent Roger Willén standing in the middle of a group of journalists who aimed their microphones at him. A cameraman was perched on top of the van, filming energetically.

"The medical examiners have found something that strengthens the suspicion of homicide, although I don't know what it is. Our colleagues in Fyrbodal have asked for backup from VGM. And you're already on the scene of course."

She heard what Hampus said, but it took a second before she reacted. "Listen, I'm on vacation! We're hunting," she exclaimed.

"You can forget about that. You're on duty instead of hunting poor, innocent moose. From what I understand the missing guy is the prime suspect."

"Or else he's also a victim," she objected quickly.

"Possibly. But we'll have to figure that out when we come up to you in a few hours. We have to finish a case before we leave."

"Okay. And here I'd hoped to avoid seeing your face for a while," she said with a theatrical sigh.

"You wish!"

Stig Ekström parked right outside the door to the shed. None of the journalists bothered to look at them, completely occupied as they were with the superintendent. The three men managed to sneak up to the door, unlock it, and slip in without anyone from the media reacting. Embla sauntered over to the group and took a place at the back to try to hear what Roger Willén was saying.

". . . any suspicions about Jan-Eric Cahneborg's death?"

"No. There is nothing that indicates that it was anything other than an accident," Willén responded.

He looked tired, with noticeable bags and dark circles under his eyes; evidently he had not slept many hours since Saturday morning. It was probably wise of him to request reinforcement from VGM, Embla thought.

Another journalist asked, "Do you have any theories about where Anders von Beehn might be found?"

"Not at this time."

"Are you continuing the search?"

"Yes, with undiminished force. We've gotten reinforcements for the search group. And as you can hear, we have a helicopter overhead, and it's equipped with a heat camera." He pointed up, and although they could hear the helicopter, it was hidden behind clouds.

"Will the frogmen continue searching in the lake?" someone asked.

"No. They're done. There was nothing to see."

The only finds were rusty old beer cans and Cahneborg's flashlight, which was in the water below the precipice. But that was not something the police intended to inform the media about.

"Is there any explanation whatsoever for von Beehn's disappearance?" one of the journalists shouted from the back row.

"No."

Before the media contingent could fire off more questions, he continued quickly. "Excuse me, but we have to go up in the forest and continue the search. I'll get back to you as soon as I know anything."

A cascade of questions came from the group. The superintendent pretended not to hear, and quickly made his way toward Embla. He passed her without stopping.

"Follow me!" he whispered from the corner of his mouth.

She immediately fell into his wake. They quickly walked toward the police car that was parked with the engine running by the logging road. This time Willén had made sure to requisition a Volvo Cross Country. Courteously he opened the back door for her. When she was in place he crawled in beside her. In the front seat were two colleagues she didn't recognize. The two young constables introduced themselves as Anette Olsson and Sebastian Jelinik. Sebastian was driving, and he took off the moment Roger Willén closed the door.

They started the slow, bumpy trip up to the Hunting Castle. The logging road had turned into pure sludge from the rain and heavy traffic. In just two days, considerably more vehicles had used the road than normally did in a year, so trying to secure any tire tracks was pointless. Presumably it would not even have been possible on Saturday, considering the rain. If they were lucky, the media representatives would stay down by the butchering shed because the road was so bad. Embla sneaked a glance at Roger Willén, who sat silently beside her. He really looked tired and worn out.

"At least it's not raining anymore," she said to try to lighten the mood.

"That's all we need," he muttered. With an audible sigh he took off his cap and ran his hand over his shaved head. After rubbing his eyes thoroughly as well he looked at her. "A number of findings have emerged from the autopsy of Cahneborg. He had a fair amount of alcohol in his system, but the most interesting thing is an impression on his back."

With some effort he got his phone out of his jacket pocket, found an image and handed the phone to her.

The photo was sharp and showed Cahneborg's sturdy back, which shimmered bluish white against the shiny steel of the autopsy table. Right below the left shoulder blade there was a distinct mark: an oblong oval with rounded ends. Given the size of the mark, it could have been inflicted with a rifle butt. A sharp shove in the back as Jan-Eric stood there up by the edge . . .

And von Beehn's rifle was missing. Like he was.

"So you think that Cahneborg got a hard hit with a rifle butt in the back?" she asked, even though she already knew the answer.

"Yes. Looks that way, doesn't it?"

It was important not to jump to the simplest explanation.

"Sure, but there's nothing that proves it was Anders von Beehn who was holding the rifle," she said.

"Then I can also tell you that the techs have compared the impression on the victim's back with the backside of the butt on a Carl Gustaf model rifle caliber 30-06. Fits exactly."

She didn't know how to respond to that. No one in her hunting party had such a rifle. On the other hand, she knew that it was not uncommon among von Beehn's hunting buddies and that it was von Beehn's favorite gun for moose hunting.

"That is a strong indication," she admitted at last.

"You might say."

"But there must be several rifle butts that fit, in terms of size. It wouldn't have to be from a Carl Gustaf," she persisted.

During the rest of the bumpy ride they sat quietly. She thought about the new information she had just received. Could this still be about a murder that was committed without prior intent? Had the two men quarreled outside the house? It was possible. No one would have heard them in the wilderness. If von Beehn really was the murderer, where could he hide? Then she had a thought.

"Listen, I'll call our colleagues at VGM. They're going to drive up here in an hour or so. I'll ask them to contact Anna. That's Stig Ekström's wife. She can let them in so they can search through Dalsnäs to be sure he's not hiding somewhere on the estate," she said.

"Good idea. But how would he have made it all the way there? It's at least fifty kilometers away."

"Well . . . He has a good and loyal manager. It was Stig Ekström who said Cahneborg and von Beehn didn't want him to come up on Friday. What if they never said that? What if Stig came here on Friday morning and picked up von Beehn, his employer?"

She could see how Superintendent Willén was racking his tired brain.

"Why would the manager lie to us?"

"Because von Beehn told him to. Maybe Stig has been bribed or threatened or something."

"Okay. Ask your colleagues to check through all the buildings at Dalsnäs."

When she took out her phone she saw there wasn't any coverage. The call would have to wait until they got to the Hunting Castle.

"Have you checked von Beehn's house in town, too?" she asked.

"Our colleagues in Stockholm have already done that and"—he interrupted himself with a big yawn—"he's not there. And if he's left the country, he would have been caught on a surveillance camera somewhere. We've already assigned people to that," he continued, stifling another yawn.

"Has anyone been in contact with the relatives? I mean both Cahneborg's and von Beehn's families."

"Oh, yes. Both the current and the ex-wives and their children hung up without saying much. Not to mention cousins, siblings, attorneys, and the devil and his grandmother!"

"No one has said they know something?"

"No. But I haven't spoken with any of them personally. Of course I'll probably have to if they come here. Which von Beehn's first wife threatened to do. Number two didn't seem too worried."

"No? Maybe she knows where he is."

"Maybe so, yes. But she's probably not going to show up here because she was on an operating table at a plastic surgeon last Friday. Replacing her silicone implants, according to a report from my colleague who spoke with her."

Embla nodded and felt no great surprise. She knew that two years earlier Anders von Beehn had remarried a woman twenty years younger. There had been a fair amount in the newspapers about the divorce from the first wife, who was a well-known opera singer and had not gone quietly.

Embla was torn out of her thoughts when the car skidded. They had to swerve around a car that was stuck far above the hubcaps in the mud.

Once at the Hunting Castle they could see that the plucky reporters and photographers had struggled all the way there on foot. They were muddy up to their knees and looked generally stressed. But Willén's arrival infused them with fresh energy, and as a group they trudged up to the police car. The superintendent got out of the car and said roughly the same things he had communicated to their colleagues outside the shed. Embla slipped out of the car door on the other side and managed to go unnoticed by the reporters. Her hunting clothes meant that she didn't look like a police officer. She went over toward the precipice, where she knew there was cell phone coverage.

When she called Hampus Stahre and asked him and Göran to stop by Dalsnäs, at first he groused and thought it sounded unnecessary. But when she told him about the mark from the rifle butt on Cahneborg's back, he changed his tune.

Then she called Nisse's cell phone. It took a few moments before he answered, and when he finally did he sounded uncharacteristically irritated.

"This is Nisse!"

"Hi there, dear uncle. I'm up at the Hunting Castle again. Superintendent Willén commandeered me to go with him. He has requested help from VGM, so I've been called back into service. Hampus and Göran are coming later this afternoon. Do you know some place they can stay?"

After thinking a moment he said, "They can stay at my place, too. I'll move in with Ingela as long as you need to be here."

"So sweet of you!"

"Think nothing of it. I may need to rest up after all this."

As she struggled not to giggle she tried to sound sympathetic. "Are they difficult? The reporters and—"

"Difficult? They're out of their minds! A crazy woman forced her way in here and started raving into a microphone: 'Here are Jan-Eric Cahneborg's and Anders von Beehn's grieving hunting comrades who, in the midst of their sorrow, have to soldier on and cut up the moose that their friends shot during the hunt.'"

"What did you say then?" She could barely keep from laughing.

"You don't want to know. But she popped out again, quick as a flash. Maybe it was mostly due to the fact that Sixten happened to drop the pail of offal over her feet."

At last she laughed heartily. It was too bad she didn't have a pail with her up here, too. Poor Willén was still stuck in the media herd. A pail of meat scraps and offal over the reporters surely would have freed him.

AT FIVE O'CLOCK Göran Krantz called and reported that he and Hampus had not found anything at Dalsnäs. There was not the slightest indication that von Beehn had been there over the past few days. His fancy Jaguar was still in the garage and some clothes were hanging in his bedroom that he had left behind for the trip home to Stockholm. Anna Ekström swore that she had not heard a word from him in a week. The last time she'd seen him was when the hunting party drove off to the Hunting Castle. Several persons were able to confirm that Stig had been at home all of Thursday and Friday, as he had helped a neighbor put on a new roof. They had worked from early in the morning until darkness fell on both Thursday and Friday. His alibi was watertight.

Embla suggested that her colleagues drive straight to Nisse's farm. They would not make it to the Hunting Castle anyway until it got dark, and there was a great risk that they would get stuck in the mud.

She called Nisse again and asked whether he and the others needed help with the meat cutting. He assured her that they were as good as done. They had called Peter Hansson and he had dropped his work at once to help them carry. Now the meat was loaded onto the wagon and they were ready to drive home.

With a feeling of relief she clicked off the call. It was nice that Peter had been able to show up on such short notice; it was certainly good for his relationship with the older men in the hunting party. And now, she reflected, that kind of thing was important to her.

Several hours after the onset of darkness Superintendent Roger Willén could see that yet another day of fruitless searching was at an end. He and Embla were in the backseat of the Volvo, with constables Olsson and Jelinik in the front. In high spirits Anette Olsson skidded down the muddy road like the worst rally driver. Embla held on as best she could to keep from hitting her head as the car swerved and careened.

"Hello, Olsson! You're driving like a fucking car thief!" Willén shouted.

The constable slowed down and took it a little easier. The passengers in the backseat could release their convulsive hold on the car interior and lean back.

"Where the hell can von Beehn be?" the superintendent said with a sigh.

"He's not anywhere around here. If he were we would have found him," said Embla.

"Yes, I believe we would have. By the way, tomorrow I need to see you and your colleagues in the Unit."

"We can meet at your office in Trollhättan. How does nine o'clock sound?"

He gave her a grateful look and a faint attempt at a smile. "Shouldn't we meet halfway? Mellerud, perhaps?"

"It's better if we meet at your office. And we have to decide where to set up the investigation center. It won't work to have it up here in the woods."

"That . . . thanks. That sounds really good. By then I'm sure we'll have managed to get news from our colleagues, who were going to question von Beehn's wife and search the house in Djursholm. And maybe the review of the images from all the surveillance cameras at trains stations and airports will have produced some results. Obviously we've also checked all reservations for trains, airlines, and boats."

"Shouldn't you put out an international search warrant?"

"Yes. If he's taken off he's certainly not inside our borders still. But my boss wants to wait and see if we produce anything before we get the big apparatus going."

The rest of the way to Nisse's farm they sat and dozed. Judging by Superintendent Willén's snoring, he was in a deeper slumber.

VGM's black Volvo XC90 was already parked on the farmyard outside the house. All the windows except the windshield were tinted so dark that it was impossible to see into the car.

When Embla opened the door to the house she was met by happy laughter. Nisse and her two colleagues, Superintendent Göran Krantz and Detective Inspector Hampus Stahre, were sitting at the kitchen table, drinking beer. The aroma of a steaming casserole in the kitchen made her realize how hungry she was.

"Hi! Come on in and sit down!" Nisse called.

He had met both Hampus and Göran on several

occasions and didn't feel the least bit uncomfortable having two policemen at his table.

"That will be nice! But I have to shower and change clothes. Stink like a beaver," she said, hurrying up the stairs to her room and the beckoning shower.

Behind her she heard Hampus ask, "Do beavers smell bad?"

Well, how would he know? Embla thought, shaking her head. Before he started at VGM his contact with nature mainly consisted of walks in Slottsskogen Park in Gothenburg.

THE CHICKEN CASSEROLE was heavenly, with the aroma and taste of garlic, chanterelles, and fresh herbs. It was impossible to resist; Embla went back for seconds. At that point Nisse had already said his goodbyes and driven off. The three colleagues had the house to themselves and while they were eating they discussed the case. Göran Krantz told them he had made contact with Ola Forsnaess's father in Oslo.

"He's old, eighty-nine. But he said something interesting. The same day that Ola went to Dalsnäs to take part in the moose hunt, he got a package. He never got to see it because he left early in the morning. But his father opened his mail a few weeks after the funeral. In the package was a gold watch, a Rolex with diamonds, but it was obviously only fool's gold and pieces of glass. Street vendors all over Asia sell knockoffs, so the watch was rather uninteresting. But there was a piece of paper with it."

Göran raised his beer glass and took a sip before he continued.

"On the paper it says, 'I remember. M.'"

"M? Is there anyone in the hunting party whose name starts with M?" Hampus asked, looking at Embla.

She shook her head and tried to recall whether anyone in the circle around the hunting party might have a name, or even nickname, starting with M, but she couldn't think of anyone.

"Does he still have those things?" she asked instead.

"Yes! He sent the package to the police station, addressed to me," said Göran.

So it was just a matter of waiting to see what the package contained. In the meantime they needed to make a more pressing decision.

Embla threw out her hands and made a gesture around the room. "Do you think it's a good idea to set up the investigation center here?"

Her colleagues exchanged a look and then they both nodded.

"Anyone who may have seen something or knows something is around here," Göran said.

"Then let's start setting things up pronto," Hampus decided.

He and Göran went out to the car and retrieved three large cases, to shore up their resources in Nisse's house. After an hour or so cables, computers, screens, a modem, a microscope, a spectrometer, and everything else they needed was set up in the room. They were used to getting organized quickly.

Besides being their boss, Göran Krantz was a trained crime scene technician and a veritable IT genius. If he had a steady supply of coffee and pastries he could sit in front of screens for hours. The three in VGM complemented each other, he liked to say. Hampus was the thoughtful, analytical one in the group. In contrast to their boss he was tall and thin—borderline skinny, in fact. His thick, dark hair had a stylish cut: short on the sides and rather long on top. When he looked at people through his round glasses he could easily pass for a stray academic and not a policeman, which had benefitted him numerous times. People were lulled into security by his harmless appearance.

As far as Embla's role in the trio was concerned, the two men usually agreed that she was their pit bull. This was said with tenderness on Göran's part and teasingly by Hampus. She didn't care. They were a good team.

"I wonder what the watch and the note mean. Who is M?" she mused out loud.

"Perhaps the note and the watch have nothing to do with this case at all. And not with Ola Forsnaess's death in a car accident either," Hampus objected.

The boss cleared his throat several times. That usually meant that he intended to announce something important.

"I have the investigation from Forsnaess's fatal accident here. He was driving his brand-new Porsche from Dalsnäs on Sunday evening in the direction of Halden. From there he would continue to Oslo. It was already rather dark but the weather was clear. The temperature was about three or four degrees Celsius and the road was dry. Forsnaess was notorious for driving too fast, and presumably he behaved no differently that evening. He drove off the road right before the border, where there's a steep descent with a sharp curve. He crashed into a tree, the Porsche was totaled, and he died immediately.

The car was equipped with an automatic emergency phone, which made it easy to find the wreck."

"That sounds like an accident to my ears. Nothing strange at all," Hampus interjected.

"Sure. But the investigation showed that there were no brake marks on the road. The car's brakes were completely flawless, so it was assumed that he must have fallen asleep at the wheel."

"A clear accident."

"Keep in mind that one of his buddies has died and another has disappeared exactly one year later," Embla noted.

"There isn't necessarily a connection," Hampus maintained.

"True. But I think the watch and note are strange. And the father has no theory at all about who M can be?" asked Göran.

At almost ninety, the father was old, Embla thought. "Does the old man seem clear in the head?" she asked.

"Crystal clear. He still works at his company."

"Can M have been a woman that Ola dumped? Maybe she sent the watch and the note as a kind of secret message between the two of them?" she suggested.

"A cheap copy of a gold watch and a cryptic note to an ex? High-strung!" Hampus said.

At last Embla felt the fatigue from the past few days kick in. She would fall asleep in her chair if she didn't go to bed. After mumbling goodnight to her colleagues she went up to her little room.

She was asleep before her head reached the pillow.

AT NINE O'CLOCK sharp the three officers from VGM strolled into the conference room that Superintendent Roger Willén had reserved for their meeting. At his side he had Constable Sebastian Jelinik and his boss, Ann-Katrin Svantesson. The police chief was a stylish woman in her fifties who was known for being both pleasant and competent. Her dark hair billowed in big, glamorous curls. Her makeup was discreet, as were her thin-framed glasses. Instead of a uniform she was wearing a short, black-and-white tunic, narrow black trousers, and high heels.

"Welcome," she said before Willén could open his mouth.

He looked a bit prickly at first but quickly recovered and put on a smile. "Hi there!" he said heartily.

A refreshing night's sleep had done miracles, his eyes radiated energy and his freshly shaved head gleamed in the glow of the fluorescent lights. His light-blue shirt was fresh and crisp.

There were several mugs, two thermoses of coffee, and a plate with a sliced tea ring in the center of the table. Göran got a warm look in his eyes when he saw the pistachio-green almond paste and the roasted almond chips;

it was his favorite pastry. While they distributed the mugs and Embla asked for hot water for tea, Ann-Katrin Svantesson started to speak.

"First I'd like to get an update. This case is getting a lot of attention in the media. I'm constantly getting inquiries about whether the investigation has produced any results. So, Roger: Has it?"

Willén cleared his throat a few times before answering. "The mark under Cahneborg's shoulder blade speaks for itself. He received a hard blow from what we have reason to believe is the butt of a rifle, and he fell down the precipice. According to the medical examiner he died immediately. The cause of death was a broken neck, which likely occurred when he struck his head on the stones below."

After a little tapping on the computer, an enlarged image of Cahneborg appeared on the wall behind him. There was a clear, violet-red mark a few centimeters below the right shoulder blade, close to the spine. The impression was angled upward, like when the hands of a clock are at five past seven.

The next tap showed a close-up of the rock by the edge of the precipice. Willén pointed at some almost-invisible marks.

"It's hard to tell in this photo, but we found scrape marks in the lichen there by the edge. Cahneborg tried to get a foothold, but as we know he didn't succeed," he said.

After a little fumbling he managed to zoom in on the edge of the cliff, so they could see the scrape marks more clearly. Embla imagined in slow-motion the sturdy Cahneborg getting a shove in the back, flailing, and desperately trying to regain his balance by seeking footing with the rough soles of his boots against the slippery lichen before falling, screaming over the edge, down to a certain death.

It was an agonizing vision and her stomach contracted in discomfort. She hadn't known him that well, but he seemed to be a fairly decent guy, although a mediocre hunter. But he was a powerful man in the media world, rich and influential. People like that always have enemies.

"Are there no traces at all of Anders von Beehn?" Ann-Katrin Svantesson asked.

"No. None at all. Apparently he went outside sometime Thursday evening or night. He took his rifle with him but not his cell phone or wallet," said Willén.

"Sounds like he intended to come right back in again," the police chief observed.

"Yes. But he didn't. And his thin clothing was hardly ideal for someone who intended to run off. If nothing else he ought to have taken a jacket. And his wallet. Perhaps he didn't want to take the phone because of the risk of being traced, but . . . Embla has said it several times and I agree with her. Something doesn't add up."

Everyone looked at her and she cleared her throat.

"I don't know von Beehn or Cahneborg that well, but I've seen them around during the past few moose hunts. I have never seen anything that can be called animosity between them. On the contrary, they always seemed really tight. And it was the same with Ola Forsnaess when he was alive. They called themselves 'the three musketeers.'" She wiggled her fingers in the air to indicate quotation marks.

"Has everyone who was there during the hunt been questioned?" Svantesson asked, looking at Willén.

"Yes. It took a little time to get ahold of them. But everyone says the same thing. There were no signs that von Beehn and Cahneborg were enemies."

There was a moment of silence before Roger Willén looked at Embla and asked, "What do you think happened?"

"No idea. But I can't believe that von Beehn would push his best friend off the precipice. I've started wondering if there was a third person at the Hunting Castle last Thursday evening."

"It's possible. But we'll have to be content with stating that von Beehn got out of bed, set aside his book, took the rifle out of the closet, put on his boots, and went out. After that we don't know what happened. But here's one more mysterious picture," the superintendent said.

A close-up of wet, muddy soil and a damp stone showed up on the wall. At first none of them saw anything noteworthy in the picture, but when Roger Willén pointed to the edge they could make out a circular impression in the muck.

"The circle is exactly seventy centimeters in diameter. There is also an unclear impression here from a sturdy boot, but only an extremely small part of the front of the sole is visible. This person was standing on the rock."

"But what is that ring?" Hampus asked.

"I don't know. Something left a very clear impression. A thin ring." He clicked again and produced a view over the precipice and the surrounding terrain.

"Cahneborg fell here . . . and here is the ring, four and a half meters from the marks on the edge."

"The lantern post is between them," Hampus noted.

"Yes. Although . . ."

The superintendent trailed off when there was a knock on the door. Constable Anette Olsson stepped in with a small package in her hand.

"Hi. An express package from the police station in Gothenburg. For you, Göran," she said.

He stood up, took the package, and immediately started removing the brown wrapping. Before he opened the thin, gray cardboard box, he put on his latex gloves. He fumbled with the tissue paper until he found what he was looking for. With a pair of long tweezers, he took hold of the metal armband and held the gleaming watch up for inspection.

"So this is a worthless copy," he said.

With some difficulty he opened a plastic bag that was on the table and put the watch in it, then he sent it around so that everyone could take a closer look. Carefully he lifted the tissue paper out of the box. At the bottom was the small slip of paper. He grasped one corner with the tweezers and placed it in a small plastic bag with a seal. He inspected the note thoroughly before he let it be passed around.

"Ordinary copy paper. Printed out on a laser printer, but I'll look more closely at that later," he said.

The piece of paper was rectangular, about five-by-seven centimeters; the lower edge was cut a bit crookedly. In the middle of the paper it said in rather large letters:

I remember. M.

Embla turned over the package but there was nothing discernable on the back: no marks, folds, or stains.

"I'll be damned!" Roger Willén exclaimed.

Ann-Katrin Svantesson gave him an astonished look and raised her eyebrows slightly.

Willén's neck was turning red and he pointed at the note. "The techs found an envelope in Cahneborg's room. Sent from Gothenburg. The address was printed out on a computer on a self-adhesive label. Self-adhesive stamps, too, so no DNA from saliva on the back side. In the envelope was a piece of fabric of some kind. And a similar note."

You could have heard a pin drop in the room. Everyone looked at him, waiting for Willén to continue, but he evidently didn't know any more than that. He feverishly tapped on the computer in front of him and let the images flicker past at a rapid pace.

"There!" he said finally.

The image showed a small, padded envelope. Beside it was a black scarf and a slip of paper. He zoomed in on the paper and everyone could see that it was identical to the one that was on the table in front of them.

"Where did they find this?" Göran Krantz asked.

"In an inside pocket of Cahneborg's suitcase." Willén sounded absent. He stood with his gaze fixed on the objects in the picture.

"A black scarf and a fake gold watch. 'I remember. M.' What is the sender trying to say?" the police chief wondered out loud. She too looked intensely at the image, as if she was trying to find something they hadn't seen at first glance.

"Probably only the sender knows that. And perhaps the recipients. That is, Ola Forsnaess and Jan-Eric Cahneborg. And neither of them can tell us anything because they're dead," Hampus said dryly.

Göran emptied the last of his coffee cup. "To me it's clear as day. Cahneborg was murdered. And we'll have to look at the investigation of Forsnaess's accident again," he said.

"Will you take that on?" Willén asked quickly.

"Sure." Göran reached for the last piece of pastry. It could be a long shift in front of the computer that afternoon, and it was crucial not to let his blood sugar sink too low.

"And what happened to von Beehn? Did he get something in the mail, too?" Ann-Katrin Svantesson looked searchingly at the police officers around the table.

Willén straightened up automatically as he answered his boss. "Right after this meeting I'm going to make contact with our colleagues in Stockholm and ask them to search his house in Djursholm one more time. Those of us who are here in the room will search through the estate and the hunting cabin in Dalsland. It will be easier now that we know what to keep an eye out for."

"We can check Dalsnäs when we drive back," said Göran.

"Good. But you can't very well drive down here every morning, can you?"

"No. It takes too much time. We've set up an operating center in a house up there. It's where Embla's uncle lives," he said.

"It was nice of him to make his house available," Svantesson said, nodding at Embla.

She knew he probably didn't have much choice, but she didn't intend to enlighten the police chief about that. Instead she simply smiled in response.

As usual Embla was driving too fast. She did not slow down until they passed a speed camera. Her colleagues let her have her way; both were sitting deeply engrossed in their own thoughts. They had had a major breakthrough during the meeting in Trollhättan.

It was Embla who said what they were thinking out loud.

"I think that Anders von Beehn's disappearance is a homicide. But there is of course a possibility that he was kidnapped."

"Murder. They have to die. All three of them," Hampus stated.

To herself she admitted that he was right. There was nothing that indicated that the perpetrator, or perpetrators, was after money. The front door to the Hunting Castle was unlocked when the manager came on Saturday morning, and von Beehn's wallet with money and all his credit cards had been lying in plain sight on top of his dresser. The same applied to Cahneborg, whose wallet was found in the drawer in the nightstand. In one of the compartments there were a couple thousand kronor in cash besides. No, this was not about money. It was personal.

"Do we know that this only concerns these three?" Göran asked thoughtfully.

"Not really. But it feels as if the musketeers are the targets," Hampus said.

Göran nodded and hummed a little. "It's getting to be lunchtime. What do you say about the Thai restaurant in Mellerud?" he said with a smile.

Hampus and Embla exchanged a look but didn't say anything. At this point they had learned the signals and what applied: pedal to the metal to whatever serving location was mentioned.

THE THAI RESTAURANT served a lunch buffet, which suited them just fine. Hampus preferred meat, Embla was picky about what she ingested, and Göran operated according to the motto "extra everything." They sat down at a window table where they could keep an eye on the car. It was conspicuous and at least twice someone had tried to break into it.

It was when she got up to fill her glass with lemon water that she noticed the solitary man at a corner table, deeply absorbed in a tabloid paper. It took her a few seconds to register who he was. His hair was considerably thinner, he was about twenty kilos heavier around the waist, and a pair of reading glasses kept slipping down his nose. He wore an elegant suit, no doubt tailor-made, of thin dark blue wool. His shirt was light blue and his silk tie was red with a tasteful white and blue checked pattern. It was many years since she'd last seen him, but this was Milo Stavic. She had no doubt about it.

For a fraction of a second Embla felt incapable of walking the short stretch across the floor over to the refrigerated case where the pitcher of water was. With an extreme exertion of will, she suppressed her sense of panic and started moving as unperturbed as she could. He did not look up from the newspaper and did not seem to notice her. Obviously he couldn't have recognized her when they came into the place. Or else he already had. The thought made cold sweat break out on her back. Because she was the only one who knew what had happened that night fourteen years ago. Besides Milo and his two brothers. And they knew more than she did.

Before the police from VGM were ready for coffee after lunch, Milo Stavic folded up his newspaper, stood up, and paid at the register. He did not even glance toward them at the window table. He probably didn't need to; she assumed he had observed them carefully when they came in. With confident steps he went up to a big, dark-blue Mercedes, started the car, and turned onto E45 without a backward glance.

She felt relieved and hoped he hadn't recognized her. Then she had been a gangly fourteen-year-old with her hair wrapped in a scarf, and she had been wearing far too much makeup. The scarf, which she had borrowed from her mother, was cobalt-blue silk and went amazingly with her eyes. She still had it and wore it often. It had hidden her conspicuous red hair, which she had scooped up in a bun on top of her head. Hopefully he hadn't made a connection between the gangly teenager and the woman who came in with two men. All three reeked of cop; an old gangster like Milo Stavic would sense that sort of thing. Maybe it was her best disguise.

After a while she managed to relax and talk more or less normally with her two colleagues.

Anna and Stig Ekström were standing outside the entry, waiting for them. The turbulence of the past few days had affected them, and they both looked tired and disheartened. Embla greeted them cheerily and chatted to lighten the mood. When she only got monosyllabic responses, she abandoned any attempts at conversation, and they went up to the carved double door.

Anna turned the key and let them in. "Do you want us to go in with you?" she asked.

"No, thanks. We'll be in touch if we need anything," Göran answered.

A faint autumn sun struggled to break through the clouds without much success, but the sparse light that filtered in through the tinted windows was sufficient enough for the furnishings in the big hall to stand out clearly: two heavy wardrobes, a large mirror with a gilded frame, a curvy rococo dresser, and a gigantic decorative rug that covered almost the entire floor surface.

"I seem to recall from my latest visit with Hampus that down here there are only rooms for entertaining, a library, and the kitchen. The bedrooms are on the top floor. It's most likely what we're looking for is there," said Göran.

"If he got an envelope or package, too, he certainly would have brought it with him to the Hunting Castle," Hampus objected.

"Probably. But we have to search here first to make sure we haven't missed anything."

Since she was inside Dalsnäs now anyway, Embla

decided to look around; neither she nor Nisse had ever been inside the big house. Quickly she walked through an impressive dining room with beautiful furniture and into a smaller living room. The room was light and peaceful, but the air was starting to acquire the smell of an uninhabited house. Tiny silver specks of dust danced in the pale rays of the sun. Big windows and a patio door faced the lake, and outside there was a large tarp draped over what was presumably garden furniture.

The library was also beautiful with its glassed-in bookshelves that hugged the walls from floor to ceiling and the well-worn leather furniture in front of the open fireplace.

Methodically, Embla started looking through the shelves and shaking all the books. The only result was that the dust made her sneeze.

For the sake of completeness she went into the kitchen. The renovation was tastefully done in a retro style.

Nothing in the house was reminiscent of the "presents" that Cahneborg and Forsnaess had received, and they did not find any notes signed M.

They reassembled in the big hall.

"We've spent almost three hours here with nothing to show for it," Hampus pointed out.

"True. To be efficient I propose that you drop me off at the farm, so I get a little time in front of the computer. It's high time to start digging more into the death of Ola Forsnaess. You two head on up to the Hunting Castle."

"It's going to be pitch black when we get there," Hampus objected.

"Aww, afraid of the dark, are you?" Embla asked him teasingly.

By the time they finally made it through the mud to the Hunting Castle, the sun had gone down. The so-called road was more like a waterlogged field. But at least it was calm and clear out.

Superintendent Willén had given them a key to the house before they left the police station in Trollhättan. He had been noticeably embarrassed about not being able to go with them or offer any extra reinforcements. His excuse was weak: "We're understaffed due to illness and parental leaves. And the investigation of a recent homicide is taking up all our resources." The murder victim was a member of a criminal gang. Such investigations are always both time-consuming and resource-draining, but Embla thought he should have been able to loan at least some of his personnel to VGM. They had a lot of ground to cover in their search.

Göran had soothed the superintendent by saying that the group was used to working independently and that they would be in touch if they needed any reinforcements. Willén was visibly relieved.

Hampus looked up toward the dark house, taking a firmer hold on the handle of his technician's bag. "The place really looks spooky," he admitted.

The windows gleamed black in the facade and the pointed gables and dormer windows of the roof stood out ghostlike against the sky. A sharp *arrk-arrk-arrk-arrk* rang out from nearby. The raven was probably drawn by the offal that had been dumped in the forest and now it was disturbed by their presence.

"Who knows, maybe Count Dracula has taken over the place!" Embla said with a laugh. But she had to admit he was right. There was something ominous about the house. She quickly composed herself and looked at Hampus. "Come on, we can't just stand here and put down roots," she said, starting to walk toward the entry.

A blast of cold struck them as the door swung open on creaking hinges. When she tried to turn on the switch nothing happened. She clicked several more times. No luck.

"Where's the fuse box?" Hampus asked.

"I have no idea."

They took their flashlights out of their jacket pockets. The beams of light flickered across the walls, but they didn't see anything that appeared to be a fuse box.

"Let's try the kitchen," he said.

They went through the hall and into the narrow corridor that led to the kitchen. He found the box behind the door. Carefully he inspected the old-fashioned porcelain fuses in the panel, then turned on the main breaker. The light in the hall came on, as did the ceiling light in the kitchen.

Embla looked around. Everything was the same since her visit together with Stig Ekström, which felt like ages ago. Even though they were indoors Hampus had not taken off his mittens and cap.

"Do they always keep it this cold here?" he complained.

"When it's not being used. It must cost a fortune to heat. Although it's strange that Stig turned off the main breaker. It really is cold as hell."

Embla's gaze fell on the door that led to the laundry room. She quickly walked across the kitchen floor and pulled the door open. They both aimed their flashlights down the long corridor. It was empty, but the backdoor that led outside stood wide open.

"No wonder it's so cold," said Hampus.

With purposeful steps Embla went up to the kitchen door. On the way she took the opportunity to shine the flashlight into the sauna and the two showers, as well as the two electric toilet stalls. All the spaces were empty. Von Beehn's and Cahneborg's jackets were hanging on separate hangers by the door, and on the hat shelf was a fur-lined cap and a pair of mittens. She swallowed hard when she saw the clothes.

Hampus closed the door and turned the lock. They switched off the flashlights and turned on the lamps in the rooms as they moved through the house.

Both of them set a course for the stairs to the top floor. They went directly into Anders von Beehn's bedroom, opened the door, and stepped in. The room was just as cold as the rest of the house. The book, glasses, wallet, and cell phone that had been on top of the dresser were gone. The techs had also taken the bedlinens and duvet with them, even though nothing indicated that a crime occurred in the room. They had taken everything with them just to be on the safe side to avoid having to come back if matters took a different turn. To put it bluntly: if von Beehn was found dead.

They started to examine the bedroom. First Embla searched in the little closet behind the wallpapered door, but there was nothing of interest. Besides a pair of old jogging shoes, the hunting vest hanging on a hook, a rifle case, and some blankets on a shelf, there was only a braided wicker wastebasket that he probably used as a gun holder. She searched for loose floorboards in the little space, but could not find any. In the meantime Hampus had rooted through the dresser with no result.

Carefully, Embla examined the horsehair-filled mattress —the only thing that was left on the bed. Nothing rustled or felt strange, and all the seams were intact. She threw it down on the floor, so she could focus on the bed itself. It was a fancy Hästens bed with a box spring that looked rather new. She lay flat on her stomach and aimed the flashlight toward the base of the bed.

"Will you help me set the bed on end?" she asked.

"It weighs a ton."

"I can handle it!"

Together they managed to move the extra-wide bed around and set it on one side. It stood steadily. Embla turned on the flashlight and started finecombing the base. Almost at once she found the tear in the fabric. It was between two wooden ribs, close the edge. When she stuck her finger in she felt a corner of something hard.

"I've found something," she said.

Hampus opened the technician's case and handed her a sturdy pair of tweezers with long pincers. She stuck the tweezers in the tear and lightly grasped the edge of what she had felt with her fingertip. Slowly she coaxed out a padded envelope: the same kind they had found in

Cahneborg's suitcase. A small plastic bag of white powder came out with it, too, and fell to the floor.

"My goodness," Hampus said, raising his eyebrows.

Shows what you know about people, she thought. She wasn't certain the substance was cocaine, but it was likely.

"We'll pick that up later. If you take out another pair of tweezers we'll check what's left in the envelope," she said.

After a little fumbling Hampus managed to fish out a key ring. No key was hanging on it—just a plastic tag.

"To a BMW," he observed.

He placed it in an evidence bag, peeked down into the envelope again, and then drew out a slip of paper.

I remember. M.

For what must be the hundredth time, he asked the question out loud.

"Who is M?"

"Not a clue. Let's go."

Outside the house the darkness was dense. They switched on their flashlights and were walking toward the car when suddenly they heard a short yelp, followed by a howl.

Hampus stopped short. "What the hell was that?"

Loudly and off-key Embla started singing the chorus to Ylvis's song "What Does the Fox Say?" When she was done she gave him a teasing look. "Now you know what the fox sounds like," she said with a laugh.

"A fox? Are you sure?"

"Absolutely. We've hunted lots of fox up here. Two years ago there was a serious outbreak of rabies, and we shot most of them. The stock hasn't really recovered yet, so we're not shooting any this season."

"Good news for the foxes."

He tried to sound cocky but she noticed he was looking around anxiously.

"On the other hand there are a number of wolves around here. They howl, but they hunt silently. You don't hear them attack," she said in a casual tone.

"Nice to know."

He walked faster and she smiled to herself as she opened the door on the driver's side and climbed in.

They had not even discussed who would drive, it was obvious that this was her territory. Embla started the car's powerful engine, and with a sigh of relief Hampus leaned back and relaxed. Slowly she started driving down the rutted road.

"Almost eight," she said after a glance at the clock on the instrument panel.

"Another day in paradise."

Hampus leaned his head heavily against the neck support. Neither of them said anything for a while. She had to concentrate on driving; it was difficult to get around the worst pools of mud. Suddenly Hampus came to life.

"Look! Taillights!" he shouted excitedly.

Embla could also make out a pair of red taillights ahead. Carefully she tried to increase speed. "The car must have come out from the road to our cabins."

"Our cabins? Which ones?"

"The hunting cabins. My hunting party. Three of them," she said between clenched teeth.

Now it was crucial to focus on driving. It was impossible to go much faster. She would have to be content if they moved forward without getting stuck in the mud.

Out of nowhere it shot out into the beam of the headlights. For a fraction of a second the fox stopped, blinded, before it leaped into the bushes and disappeared. She automatically braked hard and the car skidded. The heavy vehicle slid down into a big muddy pool by the side of the ruts. The wheels spun and dug down deep into the mud. Feverishly she tried to straighten the tires and back up, but it was fruitless. With a few audible oaths she slapped her palm on the steering wheel. Then she took a deep breath.

"You'll have to take over the wheel, I'll get out and push."

"Push? Then we'll drive right into the forest."

He was right, they would have to back the car up somehow to get back on what was supposed to be a road.

They discussed this for a while before Hampus hatched the idea that they should open one of the first aid kits that was in the car to see if there was something they could put under the tires. In each one there was a thin aluminum blanket—the kind you wrap around injured people to keep them warm. Because Embla didn't have any better suggestions they worked together to coax the blanket under the back tires as far as possible. Hampus got in the driver's seat, put the car in reverse and accelerated, while Embla pushed from the front. They had to make several attempts before they managed to get loose, and by then Embla was heavily coated with mud after slipping and falling several times.

"Damn! The taillights got away!" she moaned, trying to wipe away the mud from her hands.

"And there's no point in searching for tracks in this mud."

"Hardly."

Embla's cell phone beeped, and she reached into her pocket for her phone. A text from Peter: SEE YOU THIS EVENING? Her heart leaped and made a few extra beats, but she realized it was impossible. It would take more than an hour before they were back at Nisse's farm again. And yet another hour before she was presentable to the outside world. And she was exhausted besides. Quickly she texted: WORKING. TOMORROW? She had barely sent it before he answered, OK. XO. She found herself smiling. That was sweet. Right now she needed that.

The rest of the way they sat without speaking and listened to the radio, where Håkan Hellström kept insisting, "It will never be over for me."

AS THEY STEPPED across the threshold to Nisse's kitchen at last, Göran looked up from the computer screen. He raised his eyebrows when he saw Embla.

"Is it nice?" he asked.

"What?"

"The mudpack."

Both he and Hampus started laughing, but she was not even tempted to join in the merriment.

"That's not funny!" she snarled.

As she stomped off angrily toward the shower on the top floor he called after her, "I've made paella marinara!"

At once, she forgave him. He knew that was one of her favorite dishes.

GÖRAN HAD GOTTEN the shellfish from the frozen foods case at the ICA grocery store. There he had also shopped for saffron, olive oil, and artichoke. None of that was among the staples in Nisse's kitchen.

Over dinner they discussed the taillights they had seen on the road and the fact that the kitchen door at the Hunting Castle had been open.

"I think that the person who left the door open was also the one driving the car we saw. He, or she, was in the house when we arrived. To delay us the intruder turned off the main power switch, which provided extra time to slip out the back door," said Hampus.

"How did that person get in?" Göran asked.

"There were no marks on any of the doors. And the front door was locked when we arrived. Whoever was in there had a key," Embla asserted.

"Could it have been Anders von Beehn?"

All three thought for a few moments and came to roughly the same conclusion: it was impossible to rule that out. But why would he take the risk of returning to the Hunting Castle? If he really had killed Jan-Eric Cahneborg he would have every reason in the world to stay as far away from the scene of the crime as possible.

"I don't think it was von Beehn. If the key ring and cocaine were important, he had plenty of time to take those things with him before he split," said Hampus.

Embla nodded. "I really don't think it was him either," she said.

"So who was it?" their boss asked.

She shrugged and threw out her hands. "I have no idea. But this intruder must have gotten ahold of Anders von Beehn's keys to the cabin somehow. And the car must have been parked down the road to our hunting cabins because I didn't see it when we drove up to the Hunting Castle."

"I didn't either," said Hampus.

"So if this person walked back to the car when we arrived, there ought to be a chance of finding footprints," Göran thought out loud.

Both of his inspectors shook their heads.

"I don't think so. It's all one big muddy mess up there. Dozens of people must have tramped around there over the past few days. Not to mention all the cars . . . No, I wouldn't bother searching for footprints," said Hampus.

"What do you think about the possibility of finding fingerprints inside the house then?"

Göran looked encouragingly at them. They in turn looked at each other. Again it was Hampus who answered.

"The same problem inside the house as outside. Lots of people have streamed through it the past few days and without gloves or plastic protectors on their feet."

"So we'll have a hard time producing evidence. Then we'll have to rely on our little gray cells." Göran tapped his temple.

"Mine have already gone to bed," said Embla. She did not even try to conceal a big yawn.

"Maybe we should call it a day and get up early tomorrow," Hampus suggested.

"You do that. I'll sit here a while longer," said Göran, nodding toward the computer.

THE SIGN SAID "Staff Only." She pushed open the door and peeked in. A bare bulb shone weakly at the far end of the dark corridor. She glanced over her shoulder to check that no one on the churning dance floor was looking in her direction. Then she turned her head to assure herself that the girl at the bar was fully occupied by the customers who were hanging over the counter. Quickly she slipped in through the door and tried to close it as quietly as possible. On tiptoe she started walking toward the light. Her pulse was pounding in her ears and she had a hard time perceiving what was actually happening around her. But she must make her way to the light. Lollo was there. And presumably the others. Although she didn't want to think about them now. It was Lollo who counted, she must get her out of this place. The corridor seemed endless. The floor no longer felt solid, and her feet were sinking deeper and deeper with every step. She couldn't stop; then she would get stuck. Go on, go on! This is urgent! Lollo, I'm coming! The light came closer and through the pounding in her ears she thought she could hear voices. She saw three big shadows. They were leaning over a little, curled-up figure that she knew was Lollo. Good Lord, don't let it be too late! I will never do it again . . . Dear God . . . if you just help us! The cry she tried to let out never passed her lips, but one of the shadows suddenly turned in her direction and she realized she'd been discovered. At first she was paralyzed by fear, then she turned around to flee. But she had stopped for a fraction of a second, and that was enough. Her feet were stuck. The threatening shadow approached at a furious speed, but she was unable to move from the spot. When he came up to her she felt him take a hard grip around her throat.

"If you say a word to anybody you're dead! We know who you are and where you live!" he hissed.

Desperately she managed to force out, "Lollo, Lo—"

"Forget her!"

He threw her down on the floor. The walls around her collapsed, and she sank down into the ice-cold slime; her nostrils and mouth were covered. Breathe . . . it was impossible to breathe!

EMBLA WOKE UP when she sat up in bed and screamed. Her heart was pounding like a piston, and the sweaty T-shirt stuck to her body. *It's the same old nightmare, calm down, it's just a dream*, she exhorted herself. She took a few deep breaths and hoped she hadn't wakened her colleagues. It wouldn't be the first time if she had. They occasionally stayed in small guesthouses or hostels when they were out on a job and sometimes heard her scream. On a few occasions Göran had asked worriedly what it was that tormented her in her sleep. But she'd answered evasively, saying she'd had nightmares her whole life and didn't know why. Her boss did not look convinced, but he had never tried to press her. Perhaps he understood she was lying.

A glance at the phone showed she had only slept about an hour. It was obviously the encounter with Milo

Stavic that had provoked the dream. That man and his two brothers had been in her nightmares for fourteen years. Always the same dream: how Lollo disappeared. The worst thing was that when she woke up her childhood friend was still gone. The real nightmare never ended.

She leaned against the headboard and stared out into the darkness. Because she was wide-awake anyway she would allow herself to remember and try to go through her memories. Perhaps it would keep the dream from coming back again for a while. She didn't really think that it would ever go away for good.

She had been so proud that Lollo, who was a whole year older, wanted to be best friends with her. They lived in the same apartment building and played with each other almost every day. It had been a secure, fun childhood, as she recalled.

But the year Lollo turned fourteen everything had changed. Her father had met another woman, who was already pregnant. He would be moving to London with his new family. That was when Lollo's mother started drinking in earnest.

Lollo didn't want to talk about it, but she wasn't always able to hide how sad she was. Her depressed periods alternated with more intense ones. Over the next school year, she became restless and suggested things like smoking in secret or watching R-rated movies. As her best friend, Embla went along with it to make her a little happier.

It felt like a really cool idea when Lollo decided they should hitchhike to Copenhagen. They didn't know it at the time, but it would be their last summer vacation together. They were lucky in several senses to be picked up by a nice Danish truck driver, who believed Lollo's story that they were going to visit her grandmother. Four hours later they were standing unscathed outside Central Station in Copenhagen. From there they went to Nyhavn because the best tattoo artists were there, according to Embla's big brother, Frej.

Lollo had a little black lamb tattooed on one shoulder and Embla had chosen a blue butterfly, which she had placed high up on the outside of one thigh, where it could easily be concealed from her parents. The butterfly symbolized Lollo, her graceful figure and flighty manner. The black lamb was an image of how Embla always felt like an outsider in her family.

There was enough money for a red sausage with chopped onion, served on a paper tray, and a large Coca-Cola. With their legs dangling over the water they sat and looked at the old boats and barges that were moored along the piers. They felt free and lighthearted. And more than a little excited that they had dared to go on this adventure.

Toward evening they hitchhiked toward home again. They managed to get to Varberg, where they got kicked out of the car for refusing to have oral sex with the driver. Between the two of them, they only had sixteen kronor and fifty öre, which wasn't enough for either train or bus tickets, and they didn't dare try to hitchhike again. Dejected, they called Embla's dad to ask him to come and get them. She would never forget the scolding she got from her usually placid father. He screamed so loudly, it sounded like the phone was on speaker mode.

It had not been a fun journey home.

The news that Lollo and her mother had to move came as a cold shower. The rent for their large apartment on Linnégatan was too high. Right after Midsummer they moved to a two-room apartment in public housing in Högsbo. The only good thing about it was that it was close to the streetcar stop by Axel Dahlström's Square, and the trip was less than fifteen minutes when they wanted to meet.

It had worked pretty well. During the weeks of summer when she was with her Uncle Nisse and Aunt Ann-Sofie they called each other every day.

Not until Embla came home from Dalsland did Lollo tell her that she had met the world's sweetest guy, who was a little over twenty. Lollo herself would turn fifteen in a month; the age difference wasn't that big a deal, she said with feigned nonchalance. Embla, who had just turned fourteen, thought it probably was but was careful not to say anything; she didn't want to appear childish. She herself only had her little summer romance with Tobias to offer, and there wasn't much to talk about. He didn't even have a moped.

One Saturday afternoon at the end of August Lollo called and ordered her to dress up for a visit to a night-club that evening. After a slight panic attack—*what do you wear to a nightclub?*—Embla decided on a low-cut white tank top, black tights, and white sneakers. Because she hated her red hair at least as much as she hated her first name when she was a teenager, she wrapped one of her mother's shawls around her head. She told her parents that there was a school disco at Frölunda Cultural Center and that she and Lollo were going to have a sleepover in Högsbo afterward because it was closest. The part about the school disco at the Cultural Center was actually true, but she didn't tell them that they weren't planning to go. Nor did she mention that Lollo's mother was going to a fortieth birthday party with a girlfriend in Jönköping and would be gone for the night.

They met at Lollo's place to put on makeup and get ready. In the refrigerator there was a tub of potato salad and grilled chicken. There was also boxed white wine in the fridge, and in the pantry there were another two boxes of Spanish red wine. They chose white. Worldly wise Lollo filled two wine glasses to the brim. She assured Embla that her mother wouldn't notice anything since the box was almost full. They each had another two generously filled glasses before they left the apartment. Embla still remembered how dizzy and nauseated she had felt. She also remembered how she hoped it wasn't obvious because she didn't want to look like a wimp.

Before they left the apartment Lollo gave her an extra key in case they got separated.

The bouncers recognized Lollo and called to her. The two girls, who were obviously not twenty and evidently not sober either, got to go ahead in line outside the bar with no problem. In her slinky light-blue dress, Lollo looked like a fairy, even though she sometimes staggered alarmingly on her high heels.

The area around the bar was packed, and a dark-haired bartender had beads of sweat glistening on his forehead. A blue-haired girl worked with him and both were fully occupied. He was as lithe as a dancer behind the bar, smiling and making wisecracks with the customers while he took orders. He was good-looking, with marked cheekbones and big brown eyes that glistened when he smiled, which he did often with blindingly white teeth. His black hair was long and gathered in a thick ponytail. He was as handsome as a movie star. Lollo managed to squeeze her way up to the bar, and when he caught sight of her he lit up and walked over.

Embla herself felt lost and remained standing away from the noisy bar, so she didn't hear what they said to each other. People jostled and shouted around her. When a tipsy older guy—he was at least twenty-five—tried to hug her and insisted on a kiss she got scared and for a brief moment took her eyes off the pair at the counter. After a slight scuffle she managed to shake off the guy and moved a little farther away. When she looked toward the bar, a drunk guy was hanging over the counter, shouting for a beer. Lollo and the bartender had disappeared. The blue-haired girl bustled around alone behind the bar.

Embla started looking around, she heaved herself up on her toes and made little hops to be able to see better. People around her hissed at her not to move her arms so much. Right before the door with the STAFF ONLY sign closed, she caught a glimpse of Lollo's light-blue dress.

What happened next was the scene that constantly recurred in her nightmare. The shadow that had caught hold of Embla after she followed them through the STAFF ONLY door was Milo Stavic. She also remembered two threatening silhouettes leaning over the little figure on the floor. Later she understood that these were Milo's younger brothers, Kador and Luca. She had managed to find their names when she started working as a police officer. She had seen a photo of Luca, who was wounded in an exchange of gunfire on the Avenue, and she had recognized him at once as the good-looking bartender.

After Milo threw Embla down on the floor and went back to his brothers she lay there, gasping for breath for a long time. Half unconscious, she heard a door open and then close heavily. Somehow she managed to get up on shaky legs and stagger toward the light. All that was there was a fire extinguisher hanging on the wall beside the steel-lined outside door. The door was furnished with several locks and she wasn't able to open it; the brothers had probably locked it from the outside. She still didn't know how she made her way through the dark corridor—only that she opened a door and was swept back up in the sea of noisy, dancing people.

Somehow she ended up on a streetcar that went to Högsbo, but she had no clear memories of that ride either. Because she had a key to Lollo's apartment, it was simpler to continue to Axel Dahlström's Square than to get off at Linnégatan and try to explain to her parents why she and Lollo hadn't been at the Frölunda Cultural Center as they said. And they would notice that she was drunk. That had been the biggest reason she hadn't gone home. That and part of her hoped Lollo might be waiting for her back at her mother's apartment. And if she wasn't . . . well, Embla needed time to calmly come up with a credible lie about where Lollo was when she disappeared and why Embla didn't know where her friend had gone. Because she would never dare tell the truth. Milo Stavic's message had scared her out of her wits: "If you say a word to anyone you're dead. We know who you are and where you live!"

She had spent a wakeful night in the apartment on

Guldmyntsgatan. She was only able to fall asleep toward morning. When she woke up at lunchtime she had the first hangover of her life and felt terrible.

When she heard a key in the door a few hours later she felt a wild hope that it was Lollo, but it turned out to be her mother. Crying profusely Embla told her that Lollo hadn't come home. During the night she had fabricated a story that as far as possible tallied with the truth, but beyond that was a pure lie. Rambling a little she started by saying that Lollo had talked about a guy who lived in the city and that they were going there to meet him instead of going to the disco at the Cultural Center. She said she reluctantly went along, even though she would rather have gone to the disco. When they got off the streetcar Lollo suddenly said that she wanted to go alone to meet the guy. "You're just going to feel left out," she said. They had quarreled and she rode back to the apartment to wait for Lollo. But she never showed up. At least the latter was completely true. And no, she had no idea what the guy's name was.

She then told the same story to her parents and to the police who spoke with her a day or so later.

Afterward she rationalized her actions, telling herself she had been young and stupid. And scared. Terribly afraid! Milo had frightened her into silence. And besides, she was trying to save her own skin. There had been quite a bit of foolishness over the summer, considering the trip to Copenhagen and the tattoos. Getting drunk on wine and going to a club would hardly pass as a minor offense. She would be grounded for the foreseeable future, and she wouldn't see a whiff of an allowance for several years. She had been unable to think clearly.

Somewhere deep down she wanted to believe Lollo would come back. That everything would work out.

But it didn't. And suddenly everything was too late; too late for the truth.

Would it have made any difference if she had told someone what had really happened that evening? Yes, without a doubt. But she could not remember exactly where the club was or what it was called; she'd been too drunk. The only thing she knew for sure was that the place was called La Viva something or other. It was only much later that she figured out the club was called La Dolce Vita. She had also seen three men abduct Lollo. That would have been enough for the police to suspect the Stavic brothers because they owned the club. She knew that now, but not then.

Maybe that was why she had become a police officer. A sort of penance. Clear up all the other crimes, except the one that was already too late to solve.

Saddest of all, Lollo's mother had committed suicide the following year, with the help of a bottle of strong liquor and a vial of prescription sleeping pills.

Lollo's dad had been active in the search for his daughter to start with, but as time passed and there was no positive news he became more and more silent on the other side of the North Sea. A few years ago the TV show *Wanted* had taken up unsolved cases, and Lollo's disappearance was included. No new tips had come in.

Perhaps this was what she felt she had in common with Peter: a young teenage girl had disappeared from their lives. But it seemed to him as if his sister, Camilla, was alive. What was it he had said when she asked about his sister? "It's been a long time since we met," or something like that. That must mean she was alive, even if they don't have any contact, right? She had to try to dig deeper into that the next time she and Peter met, which if all went well would already be tomorrow evening.

The thought of him made her smile in the darkness. She crawled down under the covers, and her thoughts continued to whirl until she finally started to fall asleep. Then Peter suddenly showed up again in a waking dream. "We haven't had contact in a long time," he said, referring to his missing sister. That was what he had said, but it was a strange way to put it.

For once Göran looked really tired. He leaned his elbows heavily against the kitchen table, apathetically chewing a sausage sandwich. On top of the sausage he had squiggled mayonnaise, pressed on several slices of cucumber, and topped it with a thick slice of cheese. Hampus always teased him about his Dagwood sandwiches but realized this morning was not the time for jokes.

"Yes, please." The superintendent urgently held out his mug as Hampus came with the coffeepot to refill his own.

"This must be your third cup this morning."

"Fourth."

Without commenting, Hampus filled the outstretched mug. Embla gave her boss a searching look and noted the bags under his eyes and his uncombed hair. This was not like him. He was usually the one who was most energetic and wide-awake in the morning.

"Did you sleep at all last night?" she asked.

A faint smile appeared on his tired face. "Not much. But I have had a rewarding night on the Net."

Of course, that's where your life is, she thought.

"Can a person get the link to that site?" Hampus said with a grin.

"I was working," he said coolly. Göran took a few

substantial bites of the sandwich and drank his coffee in big gulps. The other two sat quietly; they knew he needed peace and quiet to recharge.

As usual Embla filled a plate with natural yogurt and poured her own muesli blend. Her colleagues always found that very amusing because the resulting mixture reminded them of coarse cement mortar. Then she would flex her biceps and say that they could start the day healthier, too. Hampus's part of the ritual was rolling his eyes and demonstratively spreading a thick layer of butter on a roll, while Göran reported he would go into anaphylactic shock if his poor body were subjected to anything like that.

That was the normal routine, but this morning there was none of that.

After five sandwiches and with the fifth mug of coffee in front of him on the table, Göran declared that he was ready to inform his colleagues of the results of his nocturnal labor. He nodded toward Embla.

"It was that strange sighting of the Lady in White after the hunting dinner that made me start to wonder. You found a long strand of hair at the place where you'd seen her, which you sent to me. I found that it came from a wig. Last night it struck me that we haven't looked more closely at what actually happened to Peter Hansson's sister. You said several individuals have mentioned her unusually long, light hair. I've scoured the Internet for information about her and haven't found anything. There isn't the slightest sign of life from her after she left the party that night when she disappeared thirty years ago."

"What was her name again?" Hampus asked.

"Camilla. Camilla Hansson," Embla answered quickly.

This was exactly what she herself had decided to dig into at dinner later this evening with Peter.

"With a C or a K?"

"C."

"Then she can't be M," Hampus observed.

"Actually, she could be."

They looked at Göran with surprise. *He really needs to sleep*, was Embla's first reaction.

"I happened to think of a song that was really popular when I was young. A real summertime hit. It was called "Rhythm of a Rain" or something like that. The group was called Millas Mirakel. So the girl who sang was called Milla, but her name was Camilla. With a C." His lips broke into a smile and he looked rather satisfied.

"You may be right! When I was in middle school there was a girl in the parallel class whose name was Kamilla, with a K, and she went by Millan!" Hampus exclaimed.

Embla didn't know what to say. Today Camilla would be forty-six years old and surely very unlike the sixteen-year-old who disappeared. Why would she suddenly murder three middle-aged, successful men thirty years later? She asked Göran the same question. He looked at her for a long time before he answered.

"That's what the mystery is. I decided to dig into what really happened with those three musketeers thirty years ago." In one gulp he emptied his mug and set it down on the table with a bang. "A half cup," he ordered.

This time Embla got up and scurried after the coffeepot.

"And bring a cookie!" he called after her.

When Göran had his refill and the last oatmeal cookie in the package, he continued.

"I started checking up on what those guys were up to when Camilla disappeared. Anders von Beehn was serving in the military as a coastal commando right after his university entrance exams. He was in for a year and discharged with excellent references. After that he started at Stockholm School of Economics the same autumn that Camilla disappeared. Jan-Eric Cahneborg was already there because he wasn't drafted. Ola Forsnaess doesn't seem to have done anything special during the year that von Beehn was being trained and Cahneborg started his studies. After high school he mostly travelled to various places along the Riviera and partied during the summer. When autumn came he went to Australia for three months and was in the US for the same amount of time."

He cleared his throat and sipped a little coffee before he looked at Embla.

"I want you to contact Sixten Svensson and check whether all three were at the moose hunt the year Camilla Hansson disappeared. I think he keeps lists of who participates."

"That's right. I'll talk to him," she said.

"Good. What is interesting is that the year after Camilla's disappearance, none of the three took part in the moose hunt. Ola Forsnaess and his father moved to Oslo because his mother died over the summer. Anders von Beehn went to the US and studied at a university in New York for two years before returning to the School of Economics for his final year. What is *really* interesting is that Jan-Eric Cahneborg interrupted his studies not long after the weekend Camilla disappeared. Actually just a few days later. What caught my interest was a picture from a gossip magazine taken right before Christmas that year that shows him walking through the gates to a private rehabilitation center that specializes in drug abusers. And he really looks out of it. According to the story, Jan-Eric Cahneborg, heir to Sweden's largest media empire, was admitted for several weeks of rest due to 'over-exertion'"—he made air quotes with his fingers—"but he stayed there for several months. He wasn't allowed to leave the center until almost spring. And in the fall he resumed his studies. It seems the three musketeers didn't return to the moose hunt for three years after Camilla's disappearance. Embla, can you check if that's true?"

She nodded.

"But there are quite natural explanations for why they didn't hunt," Hampus said. "I mean, studying both abroad and in Sweden, moving to Oslo, a stay at rehab . . . they had a lot going on."

"I agree. But three years is a long time. And I found some other things, too. Two years after the move to Oslo, Ola Forsnaess was charged with rape and assault—and it was brutal. The woman admitted that she went along with it to start with, but then he started slapping and strangling her. And she took a few punches as well. She said she lost consciousness toward the end of the assault. Pictures were taken at the hospital show she had been seriously battered. In short, Ola was never convicted. One of Norway's best defense attorneys acknowledged that the sex acts had been a little sadistic, but he asserted that the woman had participated voluntarily and that both of them were under the influence of drugs and the whole thing had gotten out of control. No one was surprised when the woman withdrew her report. The rumor was that daddy Forsnaess had taken out his wallet and given her a tidy sum. But the interesting thing for us is that rumors continued to circulate about Ola Forsnaess. He's mentioned on quite a few strange online forums and his name is linked to some really kinky sites. I found him both by name and by photo. It's safe to say the guy liked sadistic sex."

"Your reputation is created in cyberspace," Hampus said.

"And there it will be for eternity. Amen," Göran added. He laughed and continued. "People can try to create a facade of themselves on various social media platforms, but people like me always scare up their secret traces. It's impossible to hide anything."

He raised his coffee mug in a joking toast just as Hampus's phone started playing the theme from *The Good, the Bad and the Ugly*. With a dissatisfied grimace he read the name on the display.

"Filippa," he announced and stood up.

He didn't answer until he was out in the living room. As usual they heard his monosyllabic, curt responses. A few seconds later he came rushing back into the kitchen.

"I have to leave! Greta has been admitted to the hospital with appendicitis! She's going to have surgery . . . emergency . . . it can burst at any moment! I have to go home . . . have to take care of Ester!"

He was so upset that he stumbled over his words. Greta was four and Ester had just turned two. Of course he had to go home and take care of the younger one.

"It's okay. You can take the Veteran," Embla offered, placing a soothing hand on his shoulder.

"Not on your life! That scrap heap could fall to pieces anywhere on the road. I have to get home."

Offended on behalf of her car, she withdrew her hand. *Scrap heap, my ass!* But she had to admit that the old vehicle could be a little tricky. "Listen, I'll call Nisse. I'm sure you can use his car. They have Ingela's," she said.

She called Nisse, who promised to bring the car right away.

"No, I'll drive Hampus over to you. I'm going out anyway to talk with Sixten."

"I can go with you if you want."

"Thanks, please do."

She felt relieved. She never felt quite comfortable with Sixten; he could be extremely temperamental at times. Having Nisse along would surely facilitate contact with the old hunting leader.

THEY WATCHED HAMPUS roar off in the red Mazda and disappear in the direction of Gothenburg.

"I hope he doesn't drive off the road. I've never seen him so stressed," said Embla.

"I actually like that car," Nisse said with a sigh.

As they got into the Veteran something occurred to her that she hadn't thought of asking before.

"Has Sixten ever had a girlfriend? Or a boyfriend, for that matter."

"Boyfriend? Sixten? No. But he lived with a woman named Britt-Marie for a few years. That must have been in the early seventies. He was drinking quite a bit even then. She got fed up with it and left him."

"Does Britt-Marie still live here?"

"No. She got married and moved to Trollhättan, got a job at Saab. But she must be retired by now."

"And since then there's never been another woman?"

"No. Nothing lasting anyway. It's sad because once upon a time he was a good-looking, conscientious guy. But now . . . well, he runs the hunting party. That's something, anyway."

THEY TURNED ONTO the road to Sixten's farm. Their teeth rattled in their jaws as the car jolted along over the poorly maintained, potholed farmyard. Mud splashed around the tires.

The whole farm was dilapidated. The buildings didn't just lack a fresh coat of paint, they were all in crying need of a thorough renovation.

The rusty old tractor had stood in the same place in the middle of the farmyard for as long as Embla could remember, its wheels long concealed by brush and tall weeds. The doors to the stable were open, and in the darkness she could just make out Sixten's old green Toyota, which looked to be just as old as the Veteran. There were piles of trash everywhere, making the space resemble a small garbage dump.

"Why can't he keep things in order at his place?" Embla asked.

"You think it's messy out here? You should take a look in the barn and the old stable. And inside the house," Nisse said dryly.

She had never been inside Sixten's house; there had never been any reason. She parked the Veteran in front of the cement steps that led to the front door. Large pieces had broken loose from the steps, which would certainly be hazardous when there was snow and ice. A depressing disrepair marked the whole farm.

The same applied to its owner. When Sixten opened the door after they had knocked intensely for a long time, he looked pitiful. Thin, gray wisps of hair stuck to his head and streaks of snus were hanging in his beard stubble. He had on a soiled undershirt and a pair of dirty long underwear. His toes stuck out through thick, worn socks. The heavy stench of a hangover clung to the air. Embla felt a small shock and didn't know what she should say.

"Hi there, Sixten! Big party yesterday?" Nisse said a little teasingly.

He looks sick, Embla thought. His chest was sunken and she could see his collar bone clearly outlined under the skin. This was not the Sixten she had seen during the moose hunt, even though she had thought he smelled a little unhealthy then as well.

"What the hell do you want?" he croaked.

The gaze from his narrowed eyes was dismissive and angry. He had only cracked the door open a little.

"The police need to check the meat lists. You're known for keeping exemplary order of those."

Nisse maintained a light tone. Perhaps due to the flattery, Sixten opened the door a little more. But the surly expression did not leave his unwashed face.

"Why is that?" he snarled.

Despite the dismissive tone there was something in his body language anyway that started to change. He stuck his head out and his gaze became more present.

"It concerns who attended various hunts over the years," Nisse said evasively.

"Police secrecy," Embla quickly interjected.

Sixten's bushy eyebrows shot up and the small, bloodshot eyes reflected strong distrust. At the same time he could not really decide what this was all about, but at last curiosity took over.

"Come in then. I'll get the binders," he said.

"We'll help you carry them. There may be several," Nisse said.

"Yes? How far back do you want to go?"

So as not to reveal too much he answered deliberately vaguely. "From the mid-seventies." Then he interrupted himself, "What the hell will you . . . ?" He snorted audibly, then on unsteady legs he started walking into the house. They stepped quickly over the threshold and closed the door before he had time to change his mind.

A strong odor of cat piss and stale cooking fumes struck them. On the hall floor was a worn piece of rug that had once probably been striped in various shades of green before it had faded to gray. They went through a kitchen where all the surfaces were loaded with unwashed saucepans, china, empty TV dinner trays, cans of cat food, and empty bottles. The soles of their boots made a smacking noise as they walked across the sticky floor. None of them had taken off their footwear, which was otherwise the custom in the countryside. It was clear to Embla that he needed supervision and cleaning help, but she knew him well enough to know he would never allow anyone into the house to clean or repair anything.

They followed him into the living room, which was a faded museum of interior design from the late sixties. Almost half a century had gnawed on the sofa group's orange-brown fabric, and the tabletop had countless rings from glasses and bottles, as well as black holes from glowing cigarettes.

Sixten opened a door and gestured for them to follow him in. Embla stopped at the threshold in surprise. It was a study, furnished with an old, dark oak desk and a matching chair with curved back and velvet-covered cushion. On the desktop was a red leather blotter, an antique brass pen holder with associated inkwell, and a

Facit typewriter under a dust cover. One wall was covered by a bookcase that extended from floor to ceiling. It was dusty in the room, but an order prevailed there that was not found anywhere else on the farm.

"I work on everything that I have to take care of before the hunts in here."

Embla detected a ring of pride in Sixten's voice. Only then did she realize that the hunt was his whole life. Not in the hunting and killing itself, but in the community of the hunting party and all the work around it, the responsibility and his important task as hunting leader. He was the one who planned the hunts, and everyone had to pay attention to him and obey his orders. Maybe those were the only occasions during the year that he really got to associate with other people.

He went over to the big bookcase. "Here's where I keep the lists." His hands were shaking noticeably as he took out three thick binders. "These are from 1975 and on," he said.

"That was when you became the hunting leader," Nisse observed.

"That's right. One of the youngest ever. I took over when Pops died."

Again, she could hear the pride in his voice. He had been so young when he was shown that trust. He must have hunted a lot and been really skillful, she thought. Even if he still was a good hunting leader, it was safe to assume that now he was only a shadow of the hunter he had once been.

Sixten pointed at the desk and said, "You can sit here and look at the lists."

"We'll probably want to borrow the binders. There

may be pages we have to copy. I promise you'll get everything back no later than the day after tomorrow," Embla said.

His whole face contracted with displeasure but he did not object.

"I'll bring a couple of pilsners with me when we return them." Nisse patted his old friend on the shoulder and Sixten's expression lightened.

IT DID NOT take long to read through the meat lists, which had been meticulously kept over the years. In orderly columns Sixten had written the hunting participants' names and their allocation of meat in neat handwriting. Göran had been right in thinking that the three friends had not participated for three consecutive moose hunts in the years immediately following Camilla Hansson's disappearance.

Göran and Embla discussed whether it meant anything or if it was a coincidence. The musketeers, as they had already determined, had been occupied with other things. They agreed their absence didn't prove anything, but that they should keep it in mind during the course of the investigation.

AT LUNCHTIME EMBLA drove off to the only pizzeria in the area, Pizzeria Amore, which was adjacent to the ICA grocery store. A Vegetariano, as it had been christened on the menu on the wall, was always edible with a double portion of cabbage salad.

When the pizzas had been eaten, Göran declared that he intended to lay down for a while. Embla took the opportunity to answer several text messages from Elliot.

He was starting to get impatient and thought it was the longest hunt she had ever been on. That wasn't true; she was always gone for two weeks in connection with the moose hunt, but he could hardly remember that. She wrote back and consoled him by saying that the Water Palace in Lerum was the first place they would go when she returned to Gothenburg.

Then she tried to call Hampus, but his phone was turned off. Presumably he was at Queen Silvia's Children's Hospital with his family. KEEPING OUR FINGERS CROSSED FOR GRETA! HUGS TO ALL OF YOU! EMBLA AND GÖRAN she wrote to him.

According to the police union contract she had the right to exercise during working hours, and right now she felt it was high time for a workout. It turned out to be an intense twenty-minute conditioning session with jump rope, followed by a serious round with Nisse's punching bag and speed ball.

As always after a really hard workout she felt energetic and positive. When she came down to the kitchen after taking a shower, Göran had woken up and was making coffee and boiling water for tea. They took a break and returned to their work assignments.

Now she could no longer avoid it. She had to write the report about everything that had happened since Cahneborg's death and von Beehn's disappearance. The dates in question may span less than a week, but so much drama was involved that it felt like it had been at least a month. There was a transcription of the recording she had made when she reported to Roger Willén in Trollhättan. To save time she called the police station and got ahold of a colleague who immediately promised to send the file with her report. And because she had Trollhättan on the line anyway she asked to speak with the superintendent. After a few minutes the switchboard had found him.

"Superintendent Roger Willén."

"Hi, Embla Nyström here. I was wondering if any new lab results or other information has come in."

"Yes, actually a strange thing came in just now. In the location where we found the impression of the ring on the ground, one of the techs saw several long strands of hair hanging on a bush. The strands are evidently extremely long, and according to the techs they come from a wig," he said.

It took so long for her to respond that Willén reacted. "Hello? Are you still there?" he shouted.

"Yes, well . . . I . . . There's something that I didn't include in the report that I submitted to you."

She took a deep breath before she started telling him about her nocturnal encounter with the Lady in White. When she was done it was Willén's turn to be silent for a long time.

"I'll be damned if that's not the fishiest thing I've heard . . . And that strand of hair you found was definitely from a wig?" he said at last.

"Yes. But you see I didn't write anything about it in my report."

"Ha ha, drunk young policewoman staggers home in the night and starts seeing ghosts . . . Well, I can understand why you didn't mention it."

"I wasn't drunk. Of course I told Göran and Hampus about the Lady in White, but we didn't think it had anything to do with what happened to von Beehn and

Cahneborg. But now I'm starting to wonder. We also think we know who the M on the notes may be." She told him about Göran's connection between Camilla and the nicknames Milla or Millan.

"The rhythm of a rainy night . . . Yes, I've danced to that song many times. Millas Mirakel. Milla. M. You may have something there. The problem is we don't know where this Camilla Hansson is—or if she's even alive," said Willén.

Embla considered mentioning the evasive answer she had gotten from Peter when she asked him about his sister, but she stopped herself. "The only one who might know anything is her brother, Peter. I'm going to see him this evening. Because he works during the day, we decided to meet a little later," she said in as casual a tone as she could muster.

"Good. But it would surprise me if he knows anything about her. There are no reports that she has shown up, dead or alive, anywhere. Camilla Hansson's disappearance is now a cold case, but the case was never closed," said Willén.

After quickly deliberating with herself, Embla said, "There are actually a number of strange things that happened over the past week or so. They probably don't have anything to do with Cahneborg's death and von Beehn's disappearance, but just in case . . ."

She told him about the viper in the outhouse and the foot-hold trap the fox was caught in along the path. She also mentioned Frippe's sudden illness, which the vet determined was poisoning.

"Yeah, it's not certain that any of these things are connected, but I agree: it's strange it all happened during this particular hunt. We'll have to take all of that into account if anything else along those lines happens," said the superintendent.

As far as I'm concerned there's already more than enough strangeness, thought Embla.

LATE IN THE afternoon it started raining again. Then the wind picked up and the weather forecast warned of gusts up to twenty-five meters per second. A real storm was brewing. *Good thing we'll be indoors having a cozy evening*, thought Embla.

When she was done with the report she saw that it was time to start getting ready. Several times she caught herself smiling when she thought about the hours that were ahead of her. First a conversation about Camilla and a direct question about whether he knew what happened after her disappearance thirty years ago. After that she envisioned a repeat of Sunday evening's whirlpool bath.

Dressed in a light-blue silk tunic and narrow jeans, Embla sailed down the stairs half an hour later, surrounded by a light air of roses and jasmine. Göran whistled appreciatively.

"My, my, how gorgeous you look for this interview. Can one hope this is a permanent change of style?"

"You'd like that, wouldn't you? No, I'm going to ask Peter a few questions about his sister. And then he invited me to dinner afterward," she said smiling.

"A date?"

"One can always hope. But I promise to be back before

midnight. Then the makeup is going to disappear, I'll be dressed in my usual rags, and the Veteran will once again be . . . well, the Veteran."

They both laughed and he wished her good luck with both the questions and the date. As she passed the hat rack she grabbed an umbrella. She didn't bother with a jacket since she was just going to drive from door to door.

WHEN THE SOUND of the engine faded away and the car started to slow down, Embla screamed out loud.

"No! This can't be happening!"

The Volvo hiccupped and stopped. She simply had to accept that it had happened again: it was out of gas. But this time it was for real. She had forgotten to fill up after faking it last time. The same applied to the gas can. To top it off, she was almost two kilometers from Hansgården. When she tried to call Peter she only got his voice mail. Typical!

With a sigh, she decided to walk the last stretch. The only thing in the car that resembled a coat was a green fleece sweatshirt that she kept in the cargo space. It was old and the zipper was broken, but it was better than nothing. Besides, she did have an umbrella at least. Determinedly she stepped out into the storm, opened the hatch, pulled on the sweatshirt, and took out the two warning triangles. They were probably quite unnecessary since no one would be out on the road on a night like this, but in any event she placed one in front of the car and one behind it. Then she was ready for her unplanned walk.

The umbrella turned inside out, and the ribs broke after only a few hundred meters. Irritated, she threw the sprawling metal skeleton into the ditch. The only bright spot was that the high-heeled ankle boots, despite their glamorous appearance, were both warm and watertight. Expensive and good-looking but practical, which she was very grateful for right now. But the rest of her outfit was a total catastrophe in the storm. The tight jeans and worn fleece sweatshirt were quickly soaked. The wind bit through the silk tunic, and although she was walking at a fast pace she was starting to get stiff from the cold. The temperature hovered at around zero, but the wind chill made it feel like ten degrees below freezing. All that was missing was for the rain to turn to snow—and that actually might have been an improvement.

As she came up to the illuminated farmyard in front of Hansgården she was a wreck. The whipping rain and the headwind had not been easy to struggle against. She had managed to keep her circulation going, but when she looked down at her numb fingers she saw that two of them were starting to turn white. It was high time to get indoors.

Her hand was shaking as she reached for the clapper, but before she could take hold of it the door opened with a jerk. Of course the camera above the front door had tipped Peter off about her arrival.

"Embla! Did you walk here?" he exclaimed.

"You're not going to believe me, but the car ran out of gas again." Her teeth were chattering involuntarily as she answered.

"You'll have to jump in the whirlpool," he said firmly.

So it had to be; she did not protest. With one arm around her shoulders he piloted her toward the workout room and the beckoning Jacuzzi. She silently hoped that he would get in the tub, too. As they passed the kitchen there were delicious aromas from a cast-iron pan on the stove. On top of the stove there was also a frying pan with sizzling chanterelles.

"Venison stew," he said.

"That sounds good!"

Out in the laundry room she took off her soaking-wet clothes and hung them up in the drying cabinet. She set her phone on top of the washing machine. Then she found a thick, white terry-cloth towel and wrapped it around herself.

It was quite lovely to sink down in the warm whirlpool. Peter came in after a while and checked on her.

"I assume we'll skip the chilled champagne and go straight to tea with a splash of whiskey," he said, smiling.

"I'm completely on board with that."

Anything that could raise the temperature in her body was welcome. And she knew if he also joined her, her circulation would definitely pick up again. She leaned her head against the edge, closed her eyes, and enjoyed the massage from the warm jets. She was about to fall asleep when Peter came back with two steaming mugs, one red and one blue.

"Red for the beauty," he said, handing it to her with a smile. He sipped carefully from the blue one.

She felt a little self-conscious but asked the question anyway. "Aren't you going to get in, too?"

"Not now. Have to get the stew ready. The mushrooms still have to go in."

He smiled and set the mug down on a tall stool that was next to the tub, placed himself behind her, and gently kissed her upturned forehead. At the same time he let his hands glide across her shoulders and down toward her breasts. Carefully he caressed them. The desire grew inside her, and she was just thinking about taking hold of his arms and more or less dragging him down into the water when he suddenly stood up.

"The food. I have to check."

Before she had time to react he was on his way out of the room. *Men!* She felt disappointed and snubbed. *Don't be silly; he'll be back soon,* she admonished herself.

The tea was strong and had a sharp taste of whiskey. Because she wasn't in the habit of drinking liquor, she only dutifully took a sip of the hot drink. That would have to do. And she had to admit to herself that she already felt much better. Carefully, she set her mug beside his on the stool. With a satisfied sigh she leaned her head against the edge and closed her eyes.

"Are you asleep?"

The sound of his voice startled her.

"No. Just enjoying it."

He peeked down in her mug. "Oh, my, the naughty girl hasn't taken her medicine," he said, shaking his index finger jokingly.

"No. Alcohol's not really my thing. I drink from time to time, but there are other things that get me going," she said, winking a little teasingly.

Smiling he leaned down and gave her a long, deep kiss.

SHE WAS COMPLETELY restored after the involuntary walk in the storm. Her circulation was racing as fast as after a thorough workout, which on second thought the last half hour could be compared to. Peter proved himself to be incredibly inventive and he had great endurance. Gentle as a contented cat, she stretched in the wide bed and listened for whether he was on his way upstairs again. He had gone down to make sure the food hadn't burned.

Though she was embarrassed, she knew she had to call Nisse to ask him to come to the rescue with the gas can again. She needed her cell phone, but it was still down in the laundry room, and there was no phone in the bedroom either.

She knew her clothes would not be dry for a while and wondered if Peter had something she could borrow in the meantime. If nothing else he must have a bathrobe somewhere.

Energetically she swung her legs over the edge of the bed and went over to the nearest sliding door on the closet wall. Behind it suits, pants, and shirts were arranged neatly on hangers. There was nothing that really suited her. She closed the door and pulled open the next section. To her surprise there were no shelves and rods behind it. All she saw was a little wallpapered door flush with the wall. In the keyhole was an old-fashioned key—probably the only lock in the whole house that wasn't digital.

It was as if her hand was guided by a will of its own as it reached out and turned the key. The door glided soundlessly open. Without taking time to think, she stepped in.

The little room was a rather large side closet with a sloped ceiling. The space was faintly illuminated by what she at first perceived to be an aquarium but then realized was a large terrarium. Inside the glass a large, light-brown boa was moving slowly along a dry branch. Across the sand at the bottom of the terrarium a little black snake wriggled and slipped under a flat stone. Snakes . . . There were shelves on the walls that held a number of old things: a red enamel coffee can, a household scale, glass jars, egg cups, piles of fabric, porcelain . . . Everyday objects for the most part. Was he collecting things for a flea market? But the snakes . . .

When she twisted her head she saw the Lady in White. She was standing with her back turned toward the door facing the wall, as if she'd been put in the corner. The waist-length hair was loose and fell in a cascade down her back, and she was dressed in a white slip. A Lucia gown . . .

HER SHOULDERS HURT. Hurt like hell! The back of her head, too . . . Naked. She was naked. Cold. Nauseated. Must not vomit. There was something over her mouth. Stiff. Hard to breathe. She heard a distant moan, and it took a while before she realized that the sound came from her. Her shoulders . . . pain!

"Okay, you're starting to come to."

It was Peter's voice, but somehow not. *His* voice was warm and friendly. This one sounded sharp and cold. With an effort she cracked open her eyelids. A shadowy figure, a bright room . . . everything started whirling and she was forced to close her eyes again. She tried to get her bearings. Slowly it occurred to her that her wrists and ankles were bound. Somehow she was hanging from the ceiling. There was tape over her mouth. To gain time she let her head fall forward as if she had fainted again.

"Ugh! Fucking cop!"

That voice again, which in her dazed condition she recognized as Peter's. But what was going on? Something serious had happened. What? They'd had sex. She had gone up to his row of closets and slid a door to the side . . . behind it was another little door. Yes. She'd opened it and gone into a little room . . . snakes . . . lots of old things on shelves. The Lady in White. A secret room. A room that no one could enter. She'd gone into Peter's secret room. This was her punishment. He had beaten her and tied her up. Hung her from the ceiling. Her body ached. Crazy. He was crazy. What did he intend to do with her? Kill her? Was it really possible that he could? Why hadn't he killed her yet? Must gain time.

She was hanging heavily from her arms. With difficulty, she extended her ankles and felt her toes graze cold floorboards. As imperceptibly as possible she braced the tips of her toes against the floor. That relieved her shoulders, but she was careful not to make her hanging position look different than before. If there was anything she'd learned as a boxer, it was to sense and command the balance of her body. Now it was resting completely on her toes. That might work for a short time, but soon she would no longer have the energy.

Without moving her head she squinted. White floorboards. So she was in his office. The ceiling beams. She sensed that her wrists were bound with a sturdy yet rather soft rope—the same as around her ankles. Between her hands she could feel cold metal. A heavy-duty hook. He had hung her from a hook from one of the beams. Like the dead animals in the butchering shed. But there was a crucial difference. She was still alive, and she did not intend to give up without a fight. Now she had to figure out what he was after.

She whimpered faintly and tried to raise her head. Behind half-closed eyelids she saw him standing in front of the big computer screen on the wall. Because he had his back to her she opened her eyes completely. The whole screen was covered by a map. Google maps? Small points of light were moving extremely slowly across the map. Some were completely motionless. Only one of them was moving quickly. She was prepared when he turned around. A muffled whimper from her tape-covered mouth and a laborious attempt to open her eyes. It was important to make him believe that she was more out of it than she really was.

"As a professional snooper you're going to appreciate this. I'm keeping close track of all of you."

Triumphantly he made a gesture toward the screen. She continued to hang her head but moaned weakly. Through her eyelashes she saw him pointing toward the dots of light.

"Here's your colleague the superintendent. As usual he's sitting quietly in the house. The only time the fatso moves is when he's going to the refrigerator or the bathroom. There's your uncle. Evidently he's moved out while you all occupy his house. He's staying with a woman named Ingela Gustavsson. They've been seeing each other since last spring. But you know that because you were at her house the other evening. Karin and Björn are at home. The dot that's moving rather fast is that idiot Tobias who's out driving, and here is his dad, Einar. Even Sixten has a cell phone. Although he mostly leaves it in the house and forgets to charge it. Yes, you're probably wondering how I know all that? When I took over the farm I got the list of contact information for everyone in the hunting party, with cell phone numbers and email addresses. Thank you, thank you! It was just a matter of sending a Trojan to each and every one of you, then I was in your computers. Since then I've also been following your cell phones. I can read text messages and listen to calls."

The words just flowed out of him. That look, the polished sapphire blue. Now she realized what it was she had glimpsed when he stood with his rifle aimed at a point between Tobias's eyebrows. Pure madness.

And suddenly she understood why she always had the feeling that he could read her thoughts, how he already knew her before she had even gotten to know him. How long had he been reading her texts and emails? Could he see her browsing history? Did he understand that she was looking for Lollo?

His mouth formed a malicious grin.

"I'm sure you're wondering where your cell phone is. Why isn't it visible on the map? It no longer exists because I've neutralized it. You have ceased to exist."

With a peculiar chuckle he turned back to the computer screen and ran his fingers almost tenderly across the digital map.

"They don't know that I see and hear everything. Total control! Like I had over Forsnaess."

A sadistic glee shone in his eyes as he turned toward her again.

"His Porsche was brand new and obviously equipped with an automatic alarm. If anything happened to the car it would call for help automatically. People don't think about the fact that it's nothing but a little computer mounted in the car. It's just a matter of hacking into it. I had all the time in the world last year when you all were out in the woods hunting moose. When he came back and got in the car I was in control. I could follow exactly where he was on the screen. And he drove fast. When he came up to that sharp downhill curve I took over and put the brakes out of commission. He didn't have a chance."

Her toes were starting to ache; she knew she had to act soon. She raised her head and looked him right in the eyes. Their gazes met. Her stomach churned and she was afraid that she would throw up behind the tape. Quickly she turned her eyes away. As intended, he interpreted that to mean that she was afraid and was giving up.

"Now you're going to tell me what you and your colleagues have been up to over there in your uncle's house. Have you found any technical leads? Or anything else?"

His voice sounded treacherously smooth. She realized why she was still alive. Naturally he was afraid of having left some trace behind in or around the Hunting Castle. *Sure, just come and remove the tape from my mouth. You'll find out a thing or two.*

With the cold gaze fixed on her, he started to approach. When he was two steps from her she sharply contracted her stomach muscles, raised her knees up to her stomach and kicked toward his face with all her strength. It was his nose she was aiming at and one heel hit perfectly from below. With a crunching sound the cartilage loosened, and his head flew backward from the force of the kick. He fell back and struck his head against the edge of one of the desks. She heard a low gurgling groan as he slid down on the floor, then he was quiet. Blood streamed from his nostrils.

One of his legs was right under Embla's feet. She managed to balance on his shin while she reached up and shook her wrists loose from the hook. The rope around her wrists and ankles appeared to be a thin curtain cord; the tassels were still attached. Presumably he had it stored in his secret room. Now she saw that he had hung a tackle over the beam and hoisted her up with it. No doubt he kept that on a shelf, too.

Her feet felt numb, her toes were asleep, and her shoulders ached like hell, but she knew it was essential to get out of the house quickly before he came to. She hopped out into the hall and then carefully slid down the stairs on her butt. There was a great risk of falling if she tried to hop down. Once she had cleared the stairs, she managed to stand and made her way into the kitchen. Here there ought to be knives, but where? She started pulling out the drawers with her bound hands until she finally found the knife drawer by the stove. After several failed attempts she managed to get hold of a knife and started hacking at the rope around her ankles. Her hands were shaking and she cut herself several times, but finally she got through. Quickly she pulled the tape away from her mouth with her bound hands. It was painful and she whimpered loudly. She put the knife between her teeth and started filing on the cord that bound her hands. That did not take long, the fibers were soft. When her hands were free she threw everything to the floor except the knife, which she took with her as she stumbled off toward the laundry room.

To her relief she saw her ankle boots immediately. Even if she didn't put on any clothes, she needed something on her feet to be able to run. Because she had to run. He had guns in the house. Her half-dry clothes were hanging in the drying cabinet, but she didn't see her panties and bra, and her cell phone was gone, too. Fumbling, she started to get dressed. The jeans stuck damply to her skin but reluctantly came all the way up. She didn't bother with the tunic, it was easier to pull the damp fleece sweatshirt over her head, even though she was barely able to raise her arms. The pain in her shoulders cut like glowing iron toward her back and neck. A dull pain was pounding in the back of her head but she ignored it. She mustn't lose her head start. She didn't find her socks, but instead stuffed her bare feet into the ankle boots. She slipped over to the door and listened. She could hear sounds coming from the top floor. He must have come to. She didn't dare try to slip out through the front door; he could surely control and lock it with his codes. How would she get out? Her gaze fell on the window above the whirlpool. It was worth a try. Limping she made her way across the floor and up to the window. Latches and a lock. The lock was a problem but force could solve most things.

First by using the knife she loosened the two screws that attached the lock at the windowsill, then she guided the knife blade under the lock and pried. After a bit more coaxing she was able to remove it. An alarm started sounding somewhere in the house. She heard heavy steps on the stairs. With trembling fingers she opened the window latches and raised the window. Outside the rain was pouring as intensely as before and she could hear the harsh wind had not ceased. She set one foot on the edge of the tub and finally managed to get the other one up, too. The window was narrow but she was able to wriggle out. Headlong, she fell to the wet ground below but got up immediately. She had to quickly get away from the illuminated farmyard. She limped off toward the forest at the back of the house. He would discover that she had slipped out the window in the workout room and hopefully think she was trying to reach the road. She knew the forest like the back of her hand. She was safer there. In her mind she had a map and knew exactly which way to go. Peter's nearest neighbor was Sixten Svensson.

She was only a few meters from the protective edge of the forest when the first shot echoed. Her left upper arm throbbed heavily. While continuing to run, she checked to see if she could still move her arm. It was okay; the bullet had plowed up a flesh wound but nothing more. It was lucky he didn't have a better aim. But she couldn't take for granted that he would miss a second time. She threw herself down on the ground.

The bullet struck lower this time, she felt the splinters explode from the tree trunk in front of her. It would have hit her in the lower back. There was a brief respite while he reloaded, and she knew she had to exploit that. As a boxer she was used to ignoring pain and now she ran for all she was worth toward the nearest tree. Once there she threw herself behind the trunk and pressed herself tight against it. The shot missed and continued into the forest. Now that she was among the trees, her odds were better. There was a risk that he had a night-vision sensor on the rifle, so she decided to try to hide behind the tree trunks. She didn't need to move as fast now; the most important thing was to move in the right direction and stay out of sight. Just then she became aware of something warm running down her arm. Blood.

Embla ran in a zig-zag between the trees in what she knew was the direction of Sixten's farm. The chance that he had heard the shots was almost nonexistent. He was too far away. Besides, he was likely drunk on his ass by then. Whatever. She just needed to borrow a landline phone, not a cell phone. And hopefully a rifle. Just as she thought the word "rifle," two shots went off in close succession. Presumably he saw movements caused by the wind and was shooting at random. By this point she should be beyond his field of vision. But there was a risk that even a stray shot might hit her.

She chose to make her way to where the vegetation was densest. The rain and darkness favored her, too. In a vain attempt to stop the bleeding, she pressed her right hand hard over the wound, but she could feel the warm blood seeping through the sweatshirt.

In the darkness she could barely see her hand in front of her, and the pouring rain made the ground slippery. The last thing she needed now was a broken leg. Damp branches struck her in the face and she started getting cold again. Strangely enough she no longer felt any pain from the bullet wound, and the feeling in her toes and feet had come back, which gave her courage and renewed energy. On the final stretch to Sixten's farm she made fairly good time.

At the corner of the barn a single strong lamp lit up the yard, otherwise the farm was bathed in darkness. Was he not at home? Worst-case scenario, she would break a window. She had to get to a phone. As quietly as she could she slipped up toward the cracked front door while she looked around. All that was on the farmyard was the same scrap as before. She slipped on the broken cement step and struck her knee but barely noticed it. She felt for the door handle, and her heart jumped for joy when the door glided open while creaking in protest. Quickly she slipped in and locked the door behind her. Then she called in a hushed voice into the dark house.

"Sixten? Are you home? It's me, Embla."

She listened intensely for a response and at last picked up a sound like loud snoring from the living room. On tiptoe she went up to the doorway and peered into the darkness. Carefully she stepped into the room and approached the sofa.

"Hi, Sixten. It's Embla. I'm turning on a lamp."

From her previous visit during the day she remembered that there was a floor lamp between the sofa and one of the armchairs. Guided by Sixten's snoring she fumbled over to the lamp. It took a few moments before she found the switch, but at last she managed to turn it on. With a jerk her unintentional host woke up.

"What the hell! Who the hell . . . ?"

Confused, he laboriously sat up. The exertion provoked a wheezing coughing fit. She stood quietly and waited until it was over. He now wore a flannel shirt and a pair of old pants, but the heavy socks, wisps of hair, and streaks of snus were still there.

"It's me, Embla. I've been shot. I need to use your phone."

He wheezed and coughed again. "Shot? Who the hell shot . . . ?"

"Peter. Peter Hansson."

"Hansson! I can damn well believe it!"

Suddenly he sounded wide-awake and stone sober.

"Yes . . . Where's your phone?"

"In the kitchen. On the wall." With lightly shaking hands he rubbed his eyes and looked at her again.

"You look like hell! You're bleeding. That bastard!" he exclaimed.

But she was already on her way to the kitchen. There she turned on the ceiling light and found the phone hanging right beside the door. Clumsily she dialed Göran's cell phone number. After a few signals she heard a familiar voice.

"Superintendent Göran Krantz."

It was as if a barrier was released and the words started rushing out of her.

"It's Peter Hansson . . . he shot me! He's crazy! And armed. He's the one who killed Forsnaess and Cahneborg. He confessed to me! And he's hacked all our cell phones. He can listen to our calls and read text messages. And the emails in our computers. And he controlled Ola Forsnaess's car because it had an automatic emergency phone . . . a little computer that he hacked and . . ."

"Calm down. Where are you now?"

"With Sixten Svensson. I . . . Peter tortured me to find out how much we've figured out . . . but I managed to escape. He shot at me . . . just a flesh wound in the arm . . . it's bleeding . . ."

"I'll call for reinforcements. And an ambulance. Lock all the doors in case he comes."

Sixten was standing right behind her as she turned around. The gaze in his small, red-rimmed eyes was present. He was perhaps not quite sober but far from drunk. He had put on his hunting vest. In his hands he was holding a clean linen towel that was so heavily mangled that it cracked when he unfolded it and had a faint aroma of lavender and mothballs. Without a word he wrapped it around her wounded upper arm and fastened it with some safety pins.

"Come with me," he said, walking ahead of her toward the study.

In there he turned on the ceiling light and then went up to one of the bookshelves and started groping along the side. With a snap it moved out a little and turned on creaking hinges.

"A secret door!" she exclaimed in surprise.

"Pops made it. He was afraid of all the guns in the house. Both he and I hunt, so there were quite a few. But I follow the rules, and I've put in a real gun cabinet."

He proudly showed her the large, locked gun cabinet that was behind the bookshelf. She was truly impressed. He entered the combination and the door opened quietly. She counted eight rifles inside, along with two pistols and several stacks of ammunition on a shelf.

"Wow!"

"Yeah, you better believe we have resources here! Here, take this in case he comes after you."

He leaned forward and took out a Sako caliber 6.5

with a mounted telescopic sight. It was the rifle she was used to.

"Night-vision sensor," he said, winking.

"Super! And you?"

"I'll take my Remington. And I have a night-vision sensor for it, too."

With a grim expression he mounted the sight. Then he leaned down and took out two boxes of ammunition. One he gave to her, the other he put in one of the vest's roomy pockets. In silence they loaded their rifles.

"We'll go up to the top floor. You guard the back and I'll check the front. I'll grab the lights."

There was no trace of the grumpy old man. Straight-backed he went up to the switch to turn off the lights.

Only after the window had shattered and Sixten fell forward did she perceive the sound of the shot. As he fell his hand dragged across the switch and the ceiling light went out. Quickly Embla crouched and crawled up to the window. Without sticking her head up she fired off a shot. He answered the fire immediately, and the shot struck the lower part of the windowsill. That aroused a hope in her that he didn't have a night-vision sensor on his rifle. But the clumsy shot could also mean that he hadn't had time to mount a telescopic sight at all. She stood up and aimed toward the light that was at the corner of the barn. One shot and it turned completely dark outside. Lightning quick she crouched down again. He sent a bullet through the window but it hit high up on the wall. Right after that came another that shattered the ceiling light.

She crawled over toward Sixten. The shot had struck his left shoulder blade. He was bleeding profusely and he moaned faintly before he slipped into unconsciousness. He was old and not in the best physical shape. There was a great risk he would become Peter's next victim.

She recognized the chill that rose inside her and made her brain crystal clear. The hunting instinct.

In the kitchen the ceiling light was still on. It was crucial that he not catch sight of her through the window. She crawled on all fours across the filthy kitchen floor. Under cover of darkness in the hall she could stand up again. As carefully as she could she sneaked toward the stairs to the top floor. Something soft made her quickly move her foot and wild hissing made her heart almost stop. The cat ran like a shadow ahead of her up the stairs. After a few deep breaths to slow down her pulse she continued. Her focus was on quickly getting to the window above the study. It ought to be in the room just to the right as you came up the stairs.

The door was open. Carefully she closed it behind her, so as not to risk letting even a little light in that would expose her against the doorway.

There was a sour smell of unwashed bedlinens; she was in the bedroom. When her injured knee struck the bed-frame she swore between clenched teeth but continued up to the window. It had an old lace curtain, which suited her perfectly. Through the telescopic sight she looked toward the place where he ought to be standing. Carefully she pushed up the safety catch with her thumb. The whole time she was very careful not to graze the curtain. The slightest movement might catch his attention.

Slowly she started scanning the area through the sight. After a few seconds she saw him, shielded behind the old tractor.

Even if he performed well at the firing range under optimal conditions, the distance was too great and the night too dark for an inexperienced shooter like him. To have a chance to land a shot he would have to make his way closer to the house. He stayed close behind the tractor and offered her no good shooting angle. Sometimes he peeked out but was careful to stay behind the tractor wheels. But she could wait. That was her strength as a hunter. The icy cold was there unchanged inside her, and she knew what she had to do. He had killed three men, perhaps four if Sixten didn't recover, and he had tried to kill her. Peter was a mass murderer.

In the phosphorescent green image in the sight she saw how he wiped away the blood that was still running from his nose with what looked like a kitchen towel. He had pushed a cap down on his head as protection from the rain. He constantly looked ahead, trying to see where she was. Sometimes he directed his gaze up toward the window where she was standing, but she remained motionless.

Suddenly he was on the move and started to run in a crouch toward the house. He swerved and ran along the barn, perhaps in the hope that it would make it harder for her to locate him in the dark, but she followed him the whole time in the telescopic sight. When he stopped to peer up toward the house before he left the protection of the barn wall, she fired.

A hit in the right shoulder. The force slung him backward and he dropped the rifle. He lay there motionless by the stone base of the barn.

As quickly as she could she made her way downstairs. At the front door she stopped and turned on the light on the end of the farmhouse. To be on the safe side she put the rifle to her shoulder again and checked the sight. He was lying in the exact same position. The light barely reached the place where he was lying, but it was enough that she could orient herself without having to look in the sight as she walked. It was difficult enough to stay upright in the slippery mud in the farmyard.

When she came up she saw that he was unconscious. Bubbles of blood came out of his nostrils and he made gurgling sounds as he breathed. The blood was running from the wound in the shoulder, mixing with the mud in the puddle he had landed in. His head was leaning against the stone foundation of the barn; he must have struck the back of his head as he fell.

Presumably it was good that his head was up a little, considering the bleeding from the nose fracture. She leaned down and picked up the muddied rifle as a precaution. She did not feel anything. Inside she was empty, cold, and strangely clearheaded.

What the hell! Why did you shoot the dog?

Because it asked me to.

On shaky legs she slid her way back toward the house in the mud and managed not to fall down in the puddles.

Once she was inside the hall she locked the door, unloaded Peter's rifle, and set it in a corner. Now she could calmly walk through the kitchen and continue to the study. She turned on the desk lamp and fell on her knees beside Sixten. He moaned weakly but was still unconscious.

She remembered the cotton mittens she had seen in the gun cabinet, went for a pair, and put them on him.

At the same time she took one of the soft rags that were in a neat pile on the bottom shelf. She unscrewed the night-vision sensor on the rifle she had borrowed, carefully wiped the sight off with the rag, and set it in its box in the gun cabinet. Then she took out an ordinary sight, a Swarovski she noted automatically, and mounted it. Now the rifle she had borrowed did not have a night-vision sensor, but a regular sight. That was an important detail for the future investigation of the exchange of gunfire. Without a night-vision sensor the shot to Peter's shoulder could be deemed a random hit. If the sensor was still mounted, the shot would be harder to explain since she was known as a capable shooter within the police corps. Here it wasn't like on those American cop shows she grew up watching, where deadly force could always be excused. Swedish law was very strict where use of deadly force by the police was concerned, under any circumstances. And the last thing she wanted was an inquest into her actions—especially given how the evening had played out. No. Things were already complicated enough.

She went out in the kitchen again and wiped the cotton mittens and rag across the dirty kitchen counter. When they were really filthy she went down to the cellar with them and threw them in a corner. It would be a long time before they were discovered in the mess down there.

When that was done she went up to the hall again and took a gray raincoat down from the hanger. By the front door she took off her ankle boots and stepped into a pair of old rubber galoshes and went back out in the rain. The galoshes stuck in the gooey mud on the farmyard, and with a sucking sound the mud reluctantly released its hold. It reminded her of how she moved in the dream where Lollo disappeared. Although this was a real nightmare that she would not wake up from.

He was still lying there in the same position, exhaling bubbles and gurgling through his mouth and nose. She could not do anything about that, but she spread Sixten's raincoat over him. She ran as best she could into the house again, jumped out of the boots, and put on her ankle boots. Then she went back to the study.

Sixten had bled a lot. His respiration was weak, but he was still moaning, which meant he was alive. She took his hand and started talking to him. Presumably it was just nonsense. Afterward she didn't remember a single thing she had said.

THE VOICES ECHOED around her: "Now you're going to be poked in the arm!" "We have certain procedures for taking care of rape victims. Do you think you can cope with a gynecological examination? There are certain samples we have to take, you understand." "I'm just going to measure your pulse and blood pressure."

Everyone spoke to her in a friendly way. She nodded and mumbled affirmatively when she was expected to, and shook her head when that seemed to be appropriate, but she didn't feel like she was present.

Sometimes it felt as if she had floated up toward the ceiling. From a lookout point in one corner she gazed down on the people in the room. Unmoved she saw needles and probes being put into the body that was lying on the cot. She was indifferent about what happened to it. No, she was not there.

The physical injuries would not kill her. The gunshot wound in her arm was rather superficial and closed with a couple of stitches. The abrasions from the rope were washed clean and dressed with soft compresses and bandages. All the tears and cuts she had all over her body got the same treatment. The whole time they were testing her degree of consciousness. The bump she had on the back of her head was large and through the murmur of voices she picked up that she had a mild concussion. *Professional care*, she thought, without feeling grateful. It was as if the cold inside her would not let go. Between her and the people around her there was a thin wall of ice. It enclosed her from all sides; she found herself inside an ice cube with no way to get out. She did not know for sure if she really wanted to. Right now she was doing fine inside the cube. There were no feelings there.

Late that night she was taken to a hospital ward. A nurse gave her an injection so that she could sleep. It was marvelous to be able to slip into sleep and oblivion. Float away into nothingness.

AFTER THE MORNING rounds a psychologist stopped by. Embla assured him that she was already feeling much better and that she would soon get to speak with one of the police department's own psychologists, and she could manage until then. Of course she would need to be taken off duty immediately and go on sick leave, she added. The psychologist nodded along and then left.

Göran Krantz came to pick her up when she was discharged in the afternoon. His eyes were shiny as he gave her a cautious hug. Not even that could melt the ice inside her, but he was giving her a searching look, so she tried to smile and act normal. Presumably she wasn't able to fool him, but he didn't say anything.

When they were in the car he told her that Sixten's condition was still serious, but the doctors said he was stable. At the same time he took the opportunity to report that little Greta was doing fine and would soon be coming home from the hospital.

It was worse for Peter. He had inhaled large quantities of blood into his lungs and went into respiratory arrest right before the ambulance arrived at the hospital. He had lost a lot of blood besides due to the gunshot wound and his broken nose. And as if that weren't enough, he was struck by a massive cerebral hemorrhage and had to have emergency surgery. The blows he had incurred when he struck the back of his head twice—first against the desk and then against the stone foundation of the barn—had caused the hemorrhage. The outcome was uncertain because he was in such bad shape before surgery.

The information did not move her a bit. Not the slightest change was perceptible within the ice crystals.

Over the following days she was questioned by several different colleagues. Certain things she lied about, but she still tried to stay as close to the truth as possible.

She never intended to admit that she had willingly had sex with Peter.

She said that he raped her and assaulted her. She never intended to take back that lie. It would be a murderer's word against a policewoman whom he had tried to kill. No one would believe him.

Because several persons knew about her feelings for him, she said they had been flirting with each other since the first days of the hunt. For that reason she had been happy when he invited her to Hansgården to have dinner. She underscored that on her part it was mainly about confirming whether he knew what happened to his sister and if they'd had any contact in recent years. But the hope of a first date had been there, she admitted.

She told them about running out of gas and everything that happened after that. The injuries she had and the findings the techs made in Peter's house corroborated her story.

Both of the mugs of cold tea had still been sitting on the stool by the side of the whirlpool. The technicians found the rape drug Rohypnol in the red mug. There was no trace of any drugs in the blue mug.

Yet another lie came when they asked about the shot at Peter. She said that he was the one who had shot out the outdoor light on the barn. Sixten was wounded on the floor but she didn't dare go up to the window because Peter kept shooting in through the window of the study. In order to get a better view she had slipped up to the top floor. Despite the darkness and the rain she could still make out a movement when she looked through the telescopic sight and fired off a shot. Obviously she had aimed where she thought his legs were but unfortunately the shot hit higher up.

After ballistic investigation and a fingerprint search, they established that Peter had been shot with Embla's rifle, which did not have a night-vision sensor. Sixten's rifle had not been fired.

The conversations with the police department's own psychologist were also a balancing act on a slack line. With a tearful voice she told them how Peter had flirted with her and duped her. In retrospect she realized of course that he had just wanted to get close to her so he could stay informed about the progress of the investigation into his various crimes. The female psychologist tried to console her when she squeezed out a few tears, and to manage that she had to summon all of her acting ability.

To her worried family and all her friends she also had to playact. They invited her to dinner, came to visit with presents and flowers, sent her text messages and emails. In every way they showed that they loved her and cared about her. She sobbed and showed gratitude, exactly as was expected of her.

Played along.

But inside her everything was still quiet, cold, and dark. It felt as if her heart was surrounded by a carapace of ice. A permafrost that would never thaw.

SHE WAS ON medical leave for a week and then she was given administrative duties while the exchange of gunfire at Sixten's farm was investigated. Hampus and Göran kept her informed about the investigation. It was through them that she learned about the Rohypnol in her mug.

There had actually been several attempts at poisoning. When the veterinarian got the results from the tests he had taken on Frippe, they showed positive for glycol. Because glycol tastes sweet, dogs will eat it readily without suspecting trouble. But it is a deadly toxin and it was sheer luck that Frippe recovered without any major injury. The investigators' theory was that Peter probably gave the dog doctored sausage during the lunch break when the hunting party gathered by the grill. He had wanted to guarantee that the dog would be away from the house overnight.

Peter's secret room was pathetic. In it were a lot of things from his childhood home. You didn't need to be a psychologist to realize that he had tried to gather up the fragments of his traumatic childhood.

The Lady in White turned out to be an inflatable doll, dressed in a Lucia gown and with a long blonde wig. A black suit, with long, tight workout pants and a long-sleeved hoodie hung on another hanger. To get the doll to stay upright Peter had constructed a light metal stand that was hidden under the gown; that would explain the round impression in the soft earth by the precipice. Thanks to the stand he could easily carry the plastic doll around. He wore the black suit himself, which made him virtually invisible in the dark; it was the white female figure you saw.

In one of the albums they found a photo of Camilla, taken the year before she disappeared. Wearing a crown of lit candles, she stood at the head of her retinue of maids on the stage in an auditorium. Her eyes radiated joy, her long hair was hanging loose and glistened like spun silver. She was truly beautiful. The resemblance to Peter was clear. They had the same high cheekbones, beautiful smile, and blue eyes.

THE NIGHT BEFORE All Saints Day, Peter died. Double pneumonia had developed into general blood poisoning. The doctors were powerless. No antibiotics worked on his severe infections. At last he was pronounced dead and the respirator was turned off.

The consulting physician on the ward called Göran Krantz to ask if they had any information about his family. No relative or friend had visited him during the time he was in the hospital, and they didn't know who to contact. Göran told him how it was, namely that the police had been unable to produce the name of any close relative. He did not even have any cousins or aunts or uncles because both his parents were only children.

Embla said he had mentioned a live-in relationship

that had fallen apart. When Göran searched the addresses where Peter had been registered during the past fifteen years, there were no names listed other than his own.

An uncommonly lonely person, thought Göran. But he never shared the results of his investigations with Embla. She had enough problems of her own.

THE INVESTIGATION OF the shot that hit Peter showed that it was an unfortunate chance that Embla's shot struck him in the shoulder. But it was not the gunshot wound that was the cause of death, and she was cleared completely.

At her own request she had her final meeting with the police psychologist, who said that Embla could make contact again any time she felt the need for it. She nodded and looked grateful but knew she would never reach out. She had already crammed that nice person with enough lies.

The next day she was back at her regular duties at VGM. It had all worked out. It was over.

A FEW DAYS later, Göran made a peculiar discovery when he started going through one of Peter's computers. In an unprotected file named "The Boy Who Saw," they found a story that may have been a draft for a book. The narrator was an unnamed eight-year-old boy, but it was obvious Peter had been writing about himself. Embla read the story with a growing lump in her throat.

When she was done she swallowed several times but did not dare trust her voice, so she remained silent.

Göran looked thoughtfully at the screen. "Strange that as a security expert he didn't have a password for the file."

"As if he wanted someone to read it. An explanation. Or a cry for help," said Hampus.

Because it asked me to.

Embla cleared her throat a few times to be sure that her voice would hold.

"I'm sure you've also realized where Camilla is buried," she said.

TOGETHER WITH TWO police technicians, Hampus and Embla crawled around on the floor in the butchering shed. All four of them were equipped with flashlights and magnifying glasses. They each proceeded from a corner of the shed. Before long one of the techs shouted, "Over here!"

The other three went over to the first tech, who gestured to a group of screw heads in the floor that had fresh nicks on them that glistened in the beam of the flashlights—evidence a screwdriver had been taken to them. After a while they had a limited area that measured about one-and-a-half by two meters. With the help of a battery-operated screwdriver they quickly removed the screws and lifted up the boards. The ground below showed clear traces of having been dug up recently. Embla and Hampus took a break while the techs photographed and documented what they had found. When they were done they started digging carefully.

Both of the bodies were there. At a depth of almost one-and-a-half meters they were lying next to each other in a double grave.

FROM THE MEDICAL examiner's report it emerged that von Beehn had been buried alive. There were large quantities of dirt particles in his respiratory passages. His hands were tied behind his back with a cable tie and there was duct tape over his mouth. Beside him was his unloaded rifle. They found the ammunition under his body.

"The floorboards in the new shed weren't nailed like in the old shed but were fastened with screws instead. Peter could easily and quickly remove the floorboards. There are fresh marks on the screw heads. Because we've read his story we know how he found Camilla's grave. So he suddenly remembered what he saw in the monocular back then as an eight-year-old. As an adult he could draw certain conclusions. He probably got into the shed when it wasn't hunting season. That was no problem because as a member of the hunting party he had his own key. Once inside he had searched until he found his sister's grave. He expanded the grave, then screwed the floorboards back on," Göran said.

"So von Beehn went into the shed at gunpoint, got a blow in the head and was then placed in the grave beside the skeleton," Hampus summarized.

"That's the most-likely scenario, yes. Or else he was struck at the Hunting Castle and managed to come to again."

Buried alive. What an unbearable thought.

"And Camilla? How did she die?" Embla asked.

"There is a break on the hyoid bone, according to the medical examiner. Strangled, that is. There is also a severe fracture on the zygomatic bone on the face. And she was wearing handcuffs. Real police handcuffs."

"Ola Forsnaess," Hampus and Embla said in unison.

"Very probable, considering what we know about his sexual preferences."

Hampus grimaced and said, "And the other musketeers helped conceal his crime. One for all, and all for one!"

"Exactly. And besides that, the skeleton had a silver chain around the neck. On it was a charm in the shape of a big M."

"You were right," Embla said.

"Yes. Milla . . . And I've also found out that Peter Hansson has been a member of the Gothenburg Herpetology Society since he was fifteen."

A large, brown snake and a smaller black one flashed past in Embla's mind.

"The viper in the outhouse. I was the one he wanted to get rid of. Of course he didn't like having a police officer in the vicinity when he intended to murder two men. The night before Karin was bitten, he and I were out on a walk with the dogs and he told me he could hold the dogs in case I needed to use the outhouse. I didn't need to. And that evening Karin and I peed behind the bushes. It was pure chance that she was the one who happened to go out first that morning. It could just as well have been me. Which Peter naturally was hoping. When that didn't work he tried with the foot-hold trap. But he had bad luck again when the fox got caught in it."

When all the attacks against me failed, he bet on charm and I went for it, she thought.

She could barely conceal how sickened she felt at the thought.

When she got home to her apartment in the Kålltorp district of Gothenburg that evening she felt completely drained. She could not even bear to bend down to pick up the mail on the floor inside the door, and simply shoved it aside with her foot. She went straight to the kitchen and put on the kettle. Manually. No fiddling with a cell phone. Her home was extremely un-smart and would stay that way. She took out the tea kettle and spooned some organically grown Darjeeling into a tea strainer. While the water boiled she went to the living room and lit a few block candles that were on the coffee table. When the tea had finished steeping she took the teapot in one hand and a mug in the other. On top of the mug she set a flatbread sandwich. Total concentration was required for her to balance it all the way out to the living room. Once there she set everything down on the coffee table and collapsed onto the sofa.

As she reached for the teapot she watched without comprehending as her hand started to shake uncontrollably. The next moment the tears gushed out. She curled up on the sofa and cried openly. The ice that had been inside her cracked and in its place a black hole arose. A vacuum. An empty nothing. Helplessly she was sucked into the hole along with all the nightmare images and voices: *Peter. Sapphire gaze. I caused the injuries that killed him. The night-vision sensor. Blood. Blood! That crazy dog. Peter was a murderer. He tricked me. Idiot. I'm an idiot. And a liar. Lollo. No one must know. No one!*

The concept of time disappeared. She cried until it felt like her whole body would fall apart.

Toward the morning hours she fell asleep from pure exhaustion.

WHEN SHE AWOKE, dizzy and nauseated, she staggered over to the bathroom. The image she encountered in the mirror gave her a real shock. Her face was grotesquely swollen. She called in sick, saying she had a cold. In the freezer she had bags of frozen vegetables that she placed against her face to reduce the swelling.

ONE DAY'S ABSENCE was enough. Everything was back to normal, apart from the fact that she now had a new nightmare that haunted her. It was fused with the images from the apartment where the dog had fed on his dead master. As always she aimed toward the dog and shot it, but when she approached, the man lying in a pool of blood was Peter.

What the hell! Why did you shoot the dog?
Because it asked me to.

THE SITUATION FOR Sixten had been critical for several days, but at last he started to slowly recover. His left shoulder was totally shattered and his arm would be completely unusable in the future. The nursing staff determined it would be impossible for him to manage by himself in the house. To everyone's astonishment he let them convince him to move into municipal housing for the elderly. Rather soon he settled in and seemed more than content. The food was good, he got help with things he couldn't manage after his injury, and the staff was pleasant. Besides, he already knew most everyone who lived there. And with dinner you were allowed to have a glass of wine or a beer. It was actually not that bad.

He never mentioned a thing about the night-vision sensor that had ended up back in the locked gun cabinet. Embla hoped he had forgotten it was on the rifle she borrowed from him.

The week before Christmas she managed to find a T-shirt online with Iron Maiden and a skull, just like Elliot wanted. It was several sizes too big, but better that than too small.

The day she was going to pick up Elliot's shirt at the post office she herself got a package slip. With surprise she saw that the sender was Sixten Svensson. She had not known him to have ever given anyone a Christmas present.

It turned out to be an oblong, rather heavy but relatively small package.

Well packed in bubble wrap was the night-vision sensor.

Epilogue

"The Boy Who Saw"

The boy was awakened by loud voices that were coming from the ground floor. He realized that there was no point in trying to go back to sleep. Besides, he didn't dare to. Dad had been drinking a lot that evening. The boy knew what that usually meant.

He got out of bed, slipped over to the bathroom, and quickly got dressed.

He paused in the kitchen doorway. Mom was sitting on a kitchen chair, crying. She turned away so that he wouldn't see. Dad was standing there, looking out the kitchen window. He struck his clenched fist on the kitchen counter and said, "That goddamned little whore! When she gets home . . ."

Evidently he heard the boy's steps because he turned around and looked at him. Mom got up from the chair and wiped away her tears with the sleeve of her sweater. She tried to smile at him and said, "Millan hasn't come home yet. We're just worried . . . No one knows where she is. We've called around but no one knows . . ."

"Knock it off, damn it! She's out there with some creep

and . . ." Dad trailed off. And with another oath he turned around again and looked out into the darkness.

It would be like when his sister came home from the end-of-school party, escorted by a policeman. It was late at night and Dad had given her a hard slap. His sister and her friend had both been grounded for several weeks.

"Ninth Grade Class Party Turns into Drunken Binge." That's what it said in the newspaper. Laboriously he had read the headline word by word. In the article there had been a picture of young people sitting in the backseat of a hot rod. Some of them were hanging out of the open windows, waving. Millan was clearly holding a beer can in the photo. When Dad saw it he gave her another slap.

The boy glanced at the kitchen clock. Quarter past five was very late at night. Or early in the morning.

He felt the fear as a cramp in his throat. He managed to make it to his place at the table. But the bowl of puffed oats that Mom set in front of him was impossible to eat. The cereal floated around in the milk and slowly softened.

His chance came when Dad went to the bathroom.

Mom looked worriedly after him. "Listen . . . I'm just going to get the phone book," she whispered before she too left the kitchen.

Then he knew what he had to do. Quickly he slid down from the chair and scurried up to the freezer. He took out a bag of frozen cinnamon rolls. Three of them. That would be enough. In the refrigerator he found a bottle of pear soda. Quickly he stuffed it all in his school backpack, which was hanging inside the door to the laundry room. By the doorframe the case with the monocular was hanging on a hook. It was almost brand new and frightfully expensive. That was what Mom had said when Dad came home with it almost a year ago to the day. Frightfully expensive! Dad said that he needed it when he watched for birds. Although he never did. Mostly it hung there on the hook. The powerful monocular fit well with the boy's plan. The hook was high up, but at last he managed to get the strap loose. He put the case in the backpack. The scope was large and super heavy. It was impossible to get the zipper to work right.

Silently he slipped into the laundry room and walked toward the back door. From a hanger by the door he took down his quilted jacket. He was careful to close the door quietly so they wouldn't hear him.

It was still quite dark outside. The wind was cold. For a moment he considered going back in and getting his cap. But he didn't dare to. With cautious steps he walked toward the stable. He was not afraid, although it was very dark. He knew exactly where his bike was in the shed. The one he got as a birthday present the year before, when he turned seven. He liked it a lot. It didn't matter that it was used because it looked almost new. He groped his way toward the corner, where he knew it was waiting. He strapped the backpack on the carrier and walked the bike out. He started pedaling away toward the forest as fast as he could. He had to quickly get away from the farm. But there was probably no great risk that his parents would see him in the dark. And he had no bicycle light that could expose him.

Outside the village there were no streetlights. Here on the country road he did not see the slightest speck of light. He stopped for just a brief moment to take his mittens out of his jacket pocket. Fortunately there was a thin hood on the collar of his quilted jacket that he could pull up. It gave a little protection from the wind at least.

He wasn't allowed to be in the forest. And was absolutely not to ride off on one of the forest roads. Both Mom and Dad always said that you could easily get lost. But he remembered the big sign. If he could just see it he would find his way. He was in second grade after all and could read.

His thought was that his sister was drunk again and was hiding somewhere in the forest. Not in the little birch grove at home on the farm but in the deep forest. He understood why she wouldn't want to go home, knowing how angry Dad would be. But he would try to convince her to go with him. For Mom's sake.

Deep down he also thought that his parents would think that he had done something good. Something really brave. Because it was extremely dark in the forest. Only a brave boy dared to defy the darkness alone to search for his missing sister.

The thought livened him up and he pedaled with renewed energy. He and Dad had driven on this road right before school started. He thought that the car had moved at a snail's pace along the winding road, and he had gotten carsick but didn't dare say anything to Dad. They had driven all the way up to the steep hill. There they parked the car and climbed up to the top. Then they clambered up into the lookout tower. "This is the reward for our toil!" Dad had said, throwing out his arms.

At first the boy had been afraid because it was so high, but after a while he forgot his fear. You could see so far!

That time Dad had the monocular with him. Then it was brand new. He had shown the boy how to focus it. The boy's plan was to find where his sister was hiding with the help of the monocular. He would surely be able to see if she had gotten lost and was wandering around. She would be visible because she had her bright-pink jacket on.

He had never dared ride his bike so far away alone before. He was lost. Just as he felt he was about to start crying he heard the sound of a car engine. The car soon caught up with him and to his terror it stopped.

"Hey, kid, what are you doing out on the road this early?" he heard a familiar voice say. It was their nearest neighbor who was driving the vehicle, a small truck.

Without needing to think about it he answered, "Look . . . going to look for birds."

"Really? Do the bird brains have a youth group?" The neighbor laughed. It was not a nice laugh. Then he asked, "So where are you going to meet?"

"At . . . at the Lookout."

"The Lookout? That's a long ways away. I don't think you'll be able to bike there. But I can drive you. I'm heading that way with some material for the construction. We're working on a new butchering shed, as you know."

The boy nodded. He knew about it because Dad had helped out a little.

The neighbor tossed the bike in the back of the truck and the boy jumped up in the front seat beside him. It took a while before he caught sight of the wooden sign where someone had burned THE LOOKOUT in large letters. He remembered that sign. It was right by the path that led up to the tower. The neighbor, whose name was Sixten Svensson, stopped and dropped him off. "You have a watch. I'll come and pick you up in two hours," Sixten said.

The boy thanked him and scooted out. The neighbor helped him get the bike and the backpack down from the truck bed. With a jolt the truck disappeared down the road.

He parked the bike by the sign. Then he put on the backpack. It was super heavy. He started the climb up the path toward the lookout tower. He stumbled a few times on slippery stones and roots. Why didn't he think to bring a flashlight? The backpack was starting to feel extremely heavy and his back got sweaty. It would be lighter if he ate some of the food but he dismissed the thought. The rolls would be the reward when he had arrived.

When he reached the top he sat down by the foot of the lookout tower. The faint light meant that now he could see a little better. The sun would soon come up. Satisfied, he took the soda and the bag of rolls out of the backpack. He was the bravest person in the world who had defied the darkness alone to rescue his sister. He was a real adventurer! A hero!

He washed down the first cinnamon roll with several sips of soda. Yum! You should have a breakfast like this every day instead of wimpy puffed oats. Or boring cheese or sausage sandwiches. The roll had not really thawed in the middle, but that didn't matter. Without thinking he quickly consumed the second roll too. Now there was only half a bottle left. It was best if he saved that for the last roll. He didn't know how long he would need to be out here in the forest, looking.

Fortified by his breakfast, he climbed up in the lookout tower. It looked like an ordinary hunting tower, although higher and bigger. The local historical society had constructed it a few years earlier. He knew that Dad had been there and worked on the tower too.

Just like last time at first he thought it was awfully high when he looked out from the platform. He gripped the railing. After a while the fine view made him forget his fear of heights. The sun was on its way up. The monocular must come out of its case. It was heavy and it was harder to focus it than he remembered. The little tube that you looked in was on the top side of the device. Dad had told him to look in the tube and then he could see just fine. He found a little round screw and started turning it. After a bit he managed to get a slightly sharper image. He swept the monocular around in all directions to try to catch sight of his sister's pink jacket. If he moved the monocular too fast there was just a blur and he got dizzy, but if he stayed calm he had a clear view.

There was the butchering shed, the one Dad had shown him the year before. Although then only the foundation had been dug. It was in that shed that the hunters would cut up the moose they shot during the hunt. Although Dad had rented out his hunting right. When Sixten, who leased the land, came with the meat, Dad would usually invite him in for aquavit and beer. The last time that happened Mom hadn't said anything, but the boy saw how sad she was.

Now he tried to adjust the focus on the butchering shed. It sounded like a scary place. The butchering shed. He truly wished that Millan wouldn't be there. If she were he would have to bike the whole way there to bring her home. He would never make it. But it was a little exciting, too, of course. Some time he would dare to look more closely at that shed. Although preferably not today.

He could see the truck parked outside the shed. A man went in and out of the door with boards and boxes. The distance was too great for him to be able to see who it was, but he knew that it was Sixten Svensson. The boy watched him for a long time. He saw that the neighbor closed the door before getting into the truck again. When the boy looked at his watch there was a whole hour left before he would be picked up down by the sign. When he peeked in the little tube again he saw to his surprise that the truck was driving off right into the forest. There must be a small road, the boy assumed. But he got a little worried that the neighbor had forgotten about him. Although he did have his bike. Even if it took a little time, he would probably be able to bicycle the whole way home.

Suddenly he glimpsed something in the monocular. Something red that was moving by the side of the shed. A car. He thought he recognized that car. A BMW. Probably an E23 7 Series. He had seen it several times parked in the village. Once he had sneaked up to it and written down the make and license number in the back of his math book. He loved cars. He wanted to have a BMW like that when he got his driver's license. But this was no ordinary car in the northern parts of Dalsland. There was only one, and that was the one he had written down in his book.

It was a little blurry in the viewer, but he saw a person getting out of the car. In one hand the car key dangled with a gleaming tab on the key ring. The boy knew that it must be the BMW logo. He and his grandfather had been at a BMW dealer in Gothenburg because his grandfather also liked cars. The boy had asked if he could get such a key ring, but the salesman just laughed at him and said that he had to buy the car first.

He tried to zoom in on the key ring but it was impossible at that great distance. Besides, the monocular slipped as he supported it on the railing. The device dropped off the support and struck his knee. Fortunately it didn't fall to the floor. He set the monocular up on the railing again.

At first everything was a single jumble of colors. Disappointed, he turned the ring around the lens. There! A hand reaching for the trunk of the car. On the wrist a gold watch was gleaming in the first rays of the morning sun. The hands opened the trunk.

The boy moved the viewer a little and caught the back of another guy. He was dressed in a black T-shirt with a big skull on the back. It was impossible to read what it said but the grinning skull was clearly visible. The man in the T-shirt raised his arms and started tying a broad, black band around his head. Like a Native American. Although the hair color was wrong. Native Americans aren't blond. There was only one guy with such long blond hair in the area, and he didn't live in the area and wasn't around much. Just sometimes. He rode a big motorcycle and was a friend of the guy who owned the car. The boy in the lookout tower knew about him because it was a small community, but he didn't know what the light-haired guy's name was or the names of the other two men. There were three of them: the blond in the skull shirt, the one with the gold watch, and the one who had the keys to a BMW. It didn't seem like there were any others.

The boy aimed the monocular toward the trunk again. Now the guy who'd been driving the car was standing there, too. He put the keys in the pocket of his black leather jacket. The men were in constant motion so the boy couldn't see their faces clearly. They were too far away besides. The one who drove the car and the one with the gold watch helped each other lift a big sack out of the trunk of the car. Together they carried it into the shed. The blond took a spade and something that looked like a toolbox out of the car and followed them in and closed the door. He came right out again, started the car, and moved it behind the shed, where it was no longer visible from the road. When he had done this he went back in again.

The boy waited a long time while the men were inside the shed. He got tired and started searching the surroundings with the monocular in the hope of catching sight of the pink jacket, but he couldn't see it anywhere.

At the butchering shed nothing seemed to be happening. He

took the last drops of the pear soda and ate the roll. When he glanced at his watch he saw that he only had twenty minutes left before he was supposed to meet the neighbor again. Maybe it was best if he started walking down to the sign and the bicycle.

It was disappointing that he hadn't found his sister, but he had made an attempt. Mom and Dad would surely appreciate that.

The neighbor came almost half an hour late. He reeked of alcohol but he helped the boy load the things onto the back of the truck. He dropped the boy off at the approach to the farm. The last hundred meters he could bike himself.

"You goddamned idiot! Where the hell have you been? And with my expensive monocular!" Dad screamed as he crossed the threshold to the kitchen. With a few large strides he crossed the floor and gave the boy a slap and he fell against the doorpost.

At first the boy felt no pain. A tone started piping inside his head. At first faintly, then stronger and stronger. It was like it drowned out the pain. The fireball that formed in his chest slowly started to work its way upward and into his head. It stopped behind his eyes. He could only see the intense light. His eyes burned and he tried to rub away what hurt so much.

But then he felt the warmth that started running down his leg.

"Pear soda," he managed to think before the ball of light exploded.

The following days flowed together in a single chaos. His sister was still gone. The days turned to weeks, then months. The boy and his mother moved away from the farm and never returned.

It would take almost thirty years before he remembered what he had seen as a little boy in the monocular that morning.

Acknowledgments

THERE ARE MANY people I want to thank for all their help with this book. First and foremost a warm thanks to my publisher, Kerstin Aronsson.

Even though I have lived in Värmland for twenty-five years, my knowledge of hunting and wildlife management was extremely rudimentary before I started doing research. But I know a lot of hunters, in particular my sister Pia and brother-in-law Stefan. She read the manuscript and he patiently answered my questions. Thanks so much!

Any factual errors are entirely my responsibility and no one else's. As usual I have maintained a very loose relationship to geographic facts.

Along with the producers at Illusion Film, Johan Fälemark and Hillevi Råberg, I had already started to sketch out Åsa Embla Nyström's character in 2006 for a future film script. During the past year the author/screenwriter Stefan Ahnhem has also been involved in these discussions and contributed many valuable ideas. My very warmest thanks!

I already tested Embla in *The Treacherous Net* (Soho Crime, 2015). There she shows up in an internship and collaborates with Irene Huss and her colleagues on the Violent Crimes Unit. She worked well on the police team. Now it's time for her to stand on her own two feet. Thanks to all of you who have made that possible!

Helene Tursten